'I had to go,' she said, yet again.

'So you keep on telling me. Yet you've come back. You came to buy the house. Why?'

Majella hesitated. 'I want somewhere for myself and Grace—a place of our own. Somewhere I can begin to build a life for us.'

She turned towards him, but any words he might have said were lost when he saw her face lifted to his—skin pale and luminous as a perfect pearl in the silvery moonlight, features haloed by the dark hair.

'You're beautiful,' he said, repeating the words she'd used about the town.

She met his kiss with a heat as unexpected as it was erotic. Fierce desire coursed through him, blanking out his mind, concentrating all his being on the physical delights of touching her, holding her, feeling her skin, and flesh and bones, the scent of her filling his nostrils, hunger for her vibrating through his body.

'Flynn.'

His name fluttered off her lips and on to his, but he wasn't ready to release her yet—to stop this kiss that had shifted his world off its axis.

Meredith Webber says of herself: 'Some years ago I read an article which suggested that Mills & Boon® were looking for new medical authors. I had one of those "I can do that" moments, and gave it a try. What began as a challenge has become an obsession— though I do temper the "butt on seat" career of writing with dirty but healthy outdoor pursuits, fossicking through the Australian Outback in search of gold or opals. Having had some success in all of these endeavours, I now consider I've found the perfect lifestyle.'

Recent titles by the same author:

THE SPANISH DOCTOR'S CONVENIENT BRIDE
  Mediterranean Doctors
A FATHER BY CHRISTMAS
BRIDE AT BAY HOSPITAL
THE DOCTOR'S MARRIAGE WISH
  Crocodile Creek: 24-Hour Rescue
SHEIKH SURGEON

HIS RUNAWAY NURSE

BY
MEREDITH WEBBER

MILLS & BOON
Pure reading pleasure

First published in Great Britain 2007
Large Print edition 2007
Harlequin Mills & Boon Limited,
Eton House, 18-24 Paradise Road,
Richmond, Surrey TW9 1SR

© Meredith Webber 2007

ISBN: 978 0 263 19374 9

Set in Times Roman 16½ on 18 pt.
17-1107-54275

Printed and bound in Great Britain
by Antony Rowe Ltd, Chippenham, Wiltshire

HIS RUNAWAY NURSE

CHAPTER ONE

'THE downside of doctoring in a small country town!' Dr Flynn Sinclair muttered to himself as he pulled up behind the cluster of cars at the accident site. 'It's invariably someone you know!'

He ignored the foreboding that always gripped his gut, nodded to the policeman directing traffic around the accident, and peered at the wrecked cars, macabrely lit by the flashing red and blue lights of emergency vehicles. Neither the big four-wheel-drive nor the mangled utility were immediately recognisable but that was hardly surprising. These days both city and country folk drove four-wheel-drives while most of the young men in town considered a 'ute' with a shiny paint job as essential to their image as gelled hair and low-riding jeans.

'Flynn, over here!'

Julie, one of the local ambulance officers, waved to him from the grassy verge.

'You took your time,' she added as he drew closer.

'Twenty minutes since the call, ten to finish delivering a baby, and ten to get here,' Flynn explained, kneeling down beside the patient, young, blonde, pretty—or she was when throwing balls through hoops, not lying by the roadside covered in blood.

His heart scrunched with pain—for Becky, her parents, her entire family. Lives in turmoil.

'Becky Wainwright,' he said softly.

'I don't know her,' Julie said, 'but she's in a bad way. Single driver in the vehicle—he's fine, barely injured. Doug, my partner, is dealing with the driver of the utility. He's conscious but needs to be cut from the cabin. He had three others with him—maybe riding in the back—although they did better than Becky when he crashed.'

'Riding in the back of a ute?'

'Yeah. Stupid, isn't it? But you can't tell teenagers anything. Immortal, all of them,' Julie confirmed sadly. 'The good thing is the other three are all OK. Minor injuries—one mild concussion. Doug's got him in the ambulance already.'

Arc lights had been set up and Flynn's eyes were studying the injured girl while Julie gave her brief explanation of the other injuries then recited Becky's stats—blood pressure, respiration rate, both far too fast, fluid input, oxygen flow rate.

'We haven't dared move her while she's so unstable. I think she must have been thrown out of the ute—the passenger door had flung open and if she wasn't wearing a seat belt...'

Julie didn't need to point out the consequences, but continued, 'Possible head injuries and an open chest wound—must have landed on something sticking up from the ground.'

'Who did this?' Flynn demanded, seeing the folded material taped to Becky's chest with ordinary sticky tape.

'There was a woman here—she was in one of the first vehicles on the scene—army nurse or some such. Beads in her hair. She'd done this before we arrived and was giving mouth to mouth until we got here, and were able to hook the girl up to oxygen. I think she's seeing to the others now, or helping Doug with the driver— the army woman.'

Talking to Becky now, but eliciting no response, Flynn examined the makeshift dressing, carefully taped on three sides so on inhalation the fabric was sucked against the chest wall, sealing the wound and preventing more air entering the area around the lungs. But the woman had known enough not to tape the fourth side, which would have caused a tension pneumothorax. The dressing as it was, though makeshift and probably not sterile, acted as a flutter valve—exactly what was needed.

'She's done a good job,' Flynn admitted, adding, 'Is whatever caused the wound still in the chest?'

He glanced at Julie, who was squeezing an ambubag to assist Becky's breathing.

'The woman with the beads said she broke it off from the ground and to leave it there as moving it could cause more damage.'

'The woman with the beads was spot on,' Flynn said, lifting Becky's eyelids to check her eyes, frowning at the ovoid dilation of her right pupil, his mind racing through diagnoses, none of them good for a girl whose passion was netball, whose ambition had been to make the Aussie team.

The second ambulance officer came over.

'Can we move her?' he asked. 'There's another ambulance coming from Bendigo, ETA seven minutes. It can take the driver when the fire service blokes have disentangled him. Or if the young girl needs the city hospital it could take her and we'll wait for the driver.'

Would Becky have a better chance of survival in the regional city an hour's drive away, or even in Melbourne? Or would sending her away simply mean she'd die without her family beside her bed? The question haunted Flynn as he knelt beside the teenager, his hand clasping her wrist, feeling the pulse that raced then faltered then raced again. His probing fingers had found a depressed fracture of her skull, and whatever had pierced her chest could be causing internal bleeding. It had been thirty-five minutes since the accident—twenty-five minutes of the magic hour remaining.

Not long enough—although...

A clattering noise above them heralded the arrival of a helicopter.

'Did you call in a rescue flight?' Flynn asked Julie.

She shook her head. 'Must have been Doug, or the police.'

Or the woman with beads in her hair? She'd done everything else!

They heard the helicopter land on the emergency pad not far down the narrow winding road—a pad built because of the heavy traffic on the road during the holiday season.

'We'll send Becky down to Melbourne in the chopper,' he decided, knowing he had to give her whatever chance of survival he could, and that the helicopter would make a huge difference. Apart from the shorter trip to a major hospital, it would have emergency personnel and equipment on board which could give her better support than he could offer. 'We'll load her into your ambulance and you can transfer her to the helicopter. We won't cancel the Bendigo ambulance until we know how the driver is. If he needs to go to a regional hospital, they can take him and you can ferry the others back to Parragulla. I'll phone Becky's parents and let them know.'

Doug called to one of the policemen and the four of them lifted Becky gently onto the wheeled trolley.

'We'll carry her to the ambulance,' Flynn decreed. 'Less jolting than wheeling her over the verge. Julie, how about you go ahead and get the other passenger out? He can come to Parragulla on the next trip.'

He and Doug were slotting the trolley into position in the back of the ambulance when he heard a cry, then feet thudding along the road. He glanced around to see Ben Wainwright arguing with one of the policemen, gesticulating towards the accident—towards Flynn—a female figure racing ahead of him. There were good things about small towns as well—word got around quickly and the Wainwrights would see their daughter before she left for the city.

'How bad?'

Ben asked the question as he reached Flynn's side, his wife, Ellie, who'd run ahead, already in the ambulance, kneeling by the trolley, clasping her daughter's hand, reassuring and berating her at the same time. Then, when she got no response, reassuring only, telling her she'd be all right, promising…

'Pretty bad, Ben,' Flynn told the older man, slipping his arm around Ben's shoulders in case human contact might offer comfort. 'She must have been thrown out of the vehicle, struck her head and hit something that pierced her chest.'

'I'll kill that little turd she's been running around with. I tell you, Flynn, I'll kill him.'

'Not till you've seen Becky and Ellie through this, eh?' Flynn said gently.

Ben nodded grimly.

'There's a helicopter just down the road. I'm sending her to Melbourne,' Flynn continued. 'I don't think the rescue flight will take a passenger.' He didn't add that what they might do to Becky on the way wasn't good for a parent to be watching. 'Will you and Ellie follow in your car? Are you OK to drive? What about your other kids? Can I contact someone to look after them?'

Small-town doctor thoughts!

'I phoned Mum before we left,' Ben replied. 'She was heading over right away to stay with the young ones. She'll feed the dogs and do what has to be done. Dad'll get there when he can—he's on nightshift at the moment. Ellie's mother will probably come to Melbourne to be there for Ellie.'

'We're ready to move,' Julie called, and Ben turned to touch his wife's knee.

'I'll follow the ambulance down to the helicopter. They mightn't let you travel with her, love, but we'll drive down and be there for her when they get her settled.'

Ellie gripped his hand and nodded, and Flynn wondered at the amazing fortitude these people had summoned up, and at the strength they were apparently drawing from the love they shared. He'd seen it before, in emergency situations, yet it always struck him anew when he witnessed it.

Struck him anew and made him wonder if he would ever draw such strength from a woman.

Not so far, that was for sure!

Not that he wanted to, certain such dependence would make him vulnerable—weaken him in some way.

He, who prided himself on his strength and self-reliance, a stand he'd taken at the age of six...

Flynn asked one of the policemen to see Ben back to his car and clear the way past the accident for him, then he crossed to where a terrible shriek of metal suggested the fire department's rescue squad was getting closer to freeing the driver from the ute.

'Patrick Webster, eighteen, both legs trapped, here're the ambo's papers on him and what's been done. The other fellow—the one with concussion who was in the ambulance—is lying in the back of one of the police cars, and the other two passengers, a young girl and her brother, are in another police car.'

One of the young local constables was standing by the wrecked ute and it was he who filled Flynn in on the situation.

'I'll check them in a minute,' Flynn said, taking the sheaf of papers Doug had left with the policeman and bending to peer into the compressed and totally destroyed cabin of the smaller vehicle.

There was someone else in there—because he could see a small hand clasped against Patrick's left leg.

'Who's that?' he asked the policeman, pointing at the hand, which was all he could see of the second person.

'Army medic—first on the scene—says he's bleeding and she needs to keep pressure on his leg. She crawled through from the other side when the rescue squad cut away the door on that side.'

Flynn looked at the tangled metal and wondered how anyone—even a small person—could possibly have got into the convoluted space. But if Patrick's thigh was bleeding—femoral artery?—he needed help fast.

Streamers of silk left when the ambos had cut

away the airbags dangled around Flynn's hands and face as he leaned in to speak to Patrick and examine the trapped youth. He had a cervical collar around his neck and a small backboard supporting his spine, an oxygen mask was strapped to his face, though there was no sign of a portable tank—removed in the interests of safety while the rescue team cut away the metal—and a fluid line was taped to his right hand.

Flynn felt the lad's neck, seeking the carotid pulse, feeling the weak but steady beat. That was reassuring but Patrick's lack of response to questions was worrying.

'He was talking to us earlier,' a quiet voice said—presumably that of the army woman—the owner of the hand.

Another protesting scream of metal, and the bulk of the obstacle was finally cleared, revealing the owner of the small hand, crouched in the torn footwell on the passenger side. Face shadowed so he couldn't see the colour of her eyes or the freckles he knew were sprinkled across her nose—fairy dust old Bill had told her once when she'd complained about them...

'Majella?'

'Flynn?'

Had her name on his lips sounded as disbelieving as his had on hers?

Probably, but, with Patrick in dire trouble, this was hardly the time to be comparing levels of disbelief.

But still he stared at her, unable to believe that, after he'd searched for her for eleven months, they could meet again like this. Noticing a small scar running from the corner of her left eye, into the hairline at her temple.

Not a new scar, yet it hurt him to see this slight imperfection on her beautiful face.

'I've been putting pressure on the wound,' she said, reminding him of duty and the need for haste.

'Femoral artery?' he asked, looking at the bloody pad she held pressed against Patrick's leg.

'With luck, it's a vein,' she answered. 'There's an open fracture of his femur, and the broken bone has punctured something. I thought the best thing I could do was wrap a not-too-tight tourniquet around the leg and keep pressure on the wound while Doug handled everything else. Horrible situation. Did the chopper take the young girl?'

'Yes. She's on her way to Melbourne.'

Could he possibly be having this conversation with Majella?

Or had tiredness—Lalla Camilleri had had a very long labour—removed him to a dream state where anything was possible?

'Can you bind a new pressure pad in place so we can move him, now his feet are free?'

Surely a dream Majella wouldn't ask such a practical question.

Flynn shook his head, ridding it of the seconds of confusion, focussing on the present and the patient who needed his attention.

'You've got a clean pressure pad, Doug?' he asked the ambo, who had returned from the run to the helicopter.

Doug handed him what he needed, and Flynn slid his hand towards Majella's, asking her to lift the pad she held so he could see the blood flow from the injured vessel.

'It's not spurting, but that doesn't mean it's not the artery, leaking more inside than it is outside,' he said, almost to himself, as he looked at the slow pulse of leaking blood.

Flynn put the fresh pad into place and held it, glancing at their patient's face, asking Doug for the latest obs, trying to gauge the amount of blood Patrick had already lost and whether, with fluid running into him through a large-bore catheter, he would make the trip to the regional hospital at Bendigo, or if he'd need surgery on the torn vessel right here in Parragulla before he could be sent somewhere else.

'Are you a doctor?' he asked Majella, thinking he might be able to handle the operation if he had another doctor on hand.

She shook her head.

'Advanced paramedic training in the army, nursing skills, some emergency surgical stuff I've picked up over the years, and I can handle simple anaesthesia but if you're asking if I can repair a torn artery or vein, then no, I doubt it, although in an absolutely dire emergency I might have a go.'

Majella in the army? The Princess of Parragulla a grunt?

Disbelief flickered in the back of his mind while his medical self considered Patrick's predicament.

'It's not that dire. There are specialists in Bendigo who can handle both the blood vessel and the broken femur, but time's the thing. We need to get him on his way as soon as possible.'

Flynn had been working on a bandage to hold

the pad in place as he spoke, then was pleased to hear Doug announce the second ambulance had arrived.

'Get them up here,' Flynn told Doug. 'One of the crew will have to ride in the back, monitoring Patrick all the way and loosening the tourniquet every few minutes.'

Patrick was barely conscious, the morphine used to ease the pain during his release from the cabin of the vehicle sending him into a semi-comatose state. But Flynn spoke to him anyway, explaining what they were doing and how they were going to move him, where they would send him and what lay ahead.

He worked with the ambulance bearers to lift him out of the car, pad his legs and injured feet, splint them, then secure the lad on the trolley. Majella watched anxiously for a while, then, as he checked the oxygen flow and fluid lines hadn't been compromised in the move, and were now held securely in place, she touched his arm and said goodbye.

The ambulance doors closed behind the injured youth and Flynn looked around. Majella had disappeared.

If she'd ever been there!

Of course she'd been there! He'd seen her—spoken to her—she'd touched his arm.

He pressed his hand across the place she'd touched.

Hadn't she?

Mind back on work. He had more patients to see. What had Julie said? Three others—one with concussion from the ute and he should see the driver of the other vehicle although apparently he was OK. Flynn found the three packed into the local ambulance—the lad with concussion strapped on the trolley, his friends—a young girl who was sobbing with distress and a teenage boy who looked as if he'd like to cry but didn't want to be thought a sissy.

Flynn spoke gently to all of them, listening to their voices, checking their responses. They'd be OK until they reached the hospital.

'The other driver?' Flynn asked.

Julie shrugged.

'Gone. His vehicle was drivable. He left his name with the police and assured them he'd check with his local doctor as soon as he got home, then drove off.'

Nothing Flynn could do about that.

'I'll meet you up at the hospital,' he said, his

voice almost lost in the whine of the tow-truck crane, lifting the wrecked ute onto its tray.

He turned to head back to his vehicle as the police released the traffic that had been held up while the victims had been tended to and the road cleared. The arc lights still lit the now deserted scene, and shone on a small four-wheel-drive moving slowly up the hill towards the town—shone on the driver, a woman with beads in her hair.

A shadowy figure sat beside her—whether male or female Flynn couldn't tell. More figures were in the rear seats, another adult from the size, and a booster seat of the type that usually held a small child.

Still feeling strange—did confusion make you feel detached from reality?—Flynn made his way to his car and drove back to Parragulla, past marquees and tents that had grown like mushrooms on the showgrounds—giant mushrooms, glowing a ghostly white in the moonlight.

Festival weekend! It hadn't yet begun and already he had trouble on his hands. Trouble in the form of the accident, not Majella, although, judging by the beads, the festival was her reason for being there.

Or had she seen the ads for the auction?

He tried to remember a saying—something to do with being careful what you wish for, though he couldn't remember the consequences.

Weird! In all the ways he'd pictured a grown-up Majella over the years—and they were legion—he'd never envisaged her as either an army medic or a hippy although beaded hair didn't necessarily signify hippydom. And wasn't 'hippy' an outdated word? One he'd picked up from his mother and her friends?

But try as he may, he couldn't divert his thoughts from one person, or his mind from re-peating her name. It died to an echo then gathered strength again, nothing but her name, because he had no other thoughts to link to it—this was a woman he didn't know.

He abandoned any attempt to control his one-track mind, and continued on to the hospital. Tending patients was a sure-fire cure for a bemused, distracted brain.

As for the festival, nothing *he* could do would make it go away. He had to grin and bear it, and accept the fact that while it brought much-needed income to the town and its citizens, it also brought some very strange people to

Parragulla—including the woman he'd been seeking?—and some very bizarre medical problems more often than not.

Thinking of a past festival patient who'd imbibed oil meant for rubbing on arthritis-inflicted joints, he sighed and he pulled up in his parking space at the back of the hospital. The festival might be a time for most of the townsfolk to kick up their heels and party, but for him and his staff it was a time to hold their collective breaths and pray they'd get through it without a major disaster.

Although, with one accident already, he wasn't too hopeful.

Majella glanced towards the man standing in the middle of the road as she drove slowly past. His back was to the light so his face was shadowed, but she'd seen enough of it earlier to know Flynn hadn't changed much. Maturity and age had probably etched lines she hadn't noticed into his tanned skin, but the blue eyes still seemed to burn with passion for whatever he happened to be doing—in tonight's case saving lives—while the silky black hair still flopped onto his forehead.

'Who was that?' Helen asked, maybe sensing Majella's interest in the shadowed figure.

'Local doctor,' Majella told her, then wondered at her own evasiveness. She'd bored Helen silly in those early years, with tales of Flynn, to the extent that all three of the Sherwoods had teased her by using 'but Flynn said' as a clincher to any argument.

Those early years with Helen and Sophie and Jeff—a runaway rescued by the kindest of families! How far away they seemed. Yet as they'd driven closer to Parragulla she'd felt the shadow of the past growing heavier and heavier.

She'd known it would be hard—this return to the town of her childhood—and had decided she was mentally strong enough to handle it. But she hadn't factored Flynn into the equation. That he was a doctor had been no surprise—it had always been his ambition. But she thought he'd be long gone from the small country town— thought he'd have grown into a man too intent on being the best to be contained within its boundaries.

She took a deep breath and thought of all the reasons why she'd decided to return to the town she'd fled twelve years ago.

'Grace still sleeping?' she asked Sophie, who sat beside the three-year-old in the back of the vehicle.

'Like a baby,' Sophie joked, and Majella smiled.

All the reasons?

Never one to fool herself, Majella shook her head.

Yes, moving back to Parragulla might prove a practical solution to a number of problems, but the main reason was, and always had been, Grace. Grace, and a conviction, deep within Majella's soul, that only here, in spite of her own unhappy childhood, could she come to terms with the past, and go forward to build a happy, secure and laughter-filled home for her little daughter.

Although if Flynn was living in Parragulla— Flynn with a wife and family, Flynn as the family doctor—would it still be possible?

Of course it would be. He was a childhood friend, nothing more.

Well, nothing more than one clandestine meeting, one stolen kiss…

Friday dawned with a special radiance, as if the heavens themselves approved of the Aquarius Festival. Begun way back before Flynn's birth, it had grown from an informal annual hippy get-together to the biggest exhibition and display of natural products and alternative resources in Australia, raising the population of tiny Parragulla from one thousand souls to twenty thousand for its five-day duration.

The radiance held little delight for Flynn, peering blearily at the bit of it that was sneaking through a crack between the drawn curtains, cursing the wild cackle of the kookaburras who doubtless had had neither accidents nor dreams to disturb their sleep.

The phone had woken him—he'd promised something—now his mind stumbled to catch up with his awakening body. Festival—Majella—it's late—get to work.

'I know I'm late,' he muttered at Belle, his receptionist, as he rushed into the surgery twenty minutes later. 'If you'd had the night I had, you'd be late too!'

'I heard about the accident. How are the kids?'

Belle's voice was anxious—accidents in small country towns affected everyone in the community.

'Three are fine,' he assured her, 'and I phoned the hospitals in both Bendigo and Melbourne to check before I went to bed. Becky was still unconscious and being prepped for Theatre,

Patrick was in Theatre. That was about three a.m. so I'll phone again before I see any patients.'

'Did you get any sleep?'

Concern for him now! He found a reassuring smile for Belle, although what sleep he'd had hadn't been particularly restful. It had been dream-filled sleep—dreams of a child he'd known—a quiet child, so well behaved, for a long time he'd considered her a different species to himself, his sisters and other children he knew.

'I snatched a couple of hours,' he told Belle, remembering her question just in time. 'Then the chairman of the Festival Committee phoned to ask if I'd give the "good-bye and thank you for coming" speech at the Festival Ball on Wednesday.'

'I hope you said you would.' Belle had reverted to bossy mode, her momentary concern for him banished by her concern for Parragulla as a whole. 'Considering you got that fancy new ultrasound machine from the festival profits last year.'

'Would I dare say no?' he countered, then realised his opinion of festival time must have been written on his face for she gave him a stern look.

'When you were a boy, you were always saying you wanted to see the world,' she reminded him. 'Well, at festival time the world comes to you. And the money from it does a lot of good in this town—remember that.'

'It's not the festival I object to, it's the people it attracts!' he grumbled, more upset by the echo persisting in his head—the woman's name— than Belle's scolding. He pushed through the door that led to his private office.

'She might be dead. Have you thought of that?'

He'd sensed rather than heard Belle following him into the office, but it was her statement not her presence that shook him.

'Who might be dead?' he demanded, and she gave him one of those infuriating women-know-everything looks.

'The woman you've been looking for— Majella,' she said calmly, and Flynn dropped into his chair and stared at Belle in disbelief as she continued without missing a beat. 'She was fifteen, Flynn, when she ran away. Where would she go? Who would she turn to? A protected, cosseted kid like that—where would she end up but on the streets?'

And hearing Belle put the bleakest of his own thoughts into words, his heart faltered momentarily—then he remembered.

'Well, she's not dead,' he said, and took delight in the shock on Belle's face. Belle prided herself on being the first to know everything that happened in Parragulla. 'She's alive and well, and, I suspect, right here in Parragulla.'

'You found her?' Disbelief vied with delight in Belle's voice.

'She found herself,' Flynn replied, aware his own contrary reaction to Majella's return might, at least in part, be to do with the fact that the woman he'd been searching for had turned up of her own accord.

Unless she'd seen the ad…

'But that's wonderful. Have you spoken to her? Do you know why she ran away? Was she pregnant like her mother was when she ran away? She was about the same age. I wonder if she kept the child? It'd be, what—eleven or twelve by now.'

'She wasn't pregnant when she ran away!'

Stupid thing to say to Belle! She'd want to know how he knew, and it was impossible to explain his conviction—to put into words the sweet and gentle innocence of the young Majella who'd trembled in his arms that strange, almost dreamlike night he'd finally kissed her.

'You can't know that,' Belle protested, right on cue. 'Oh, I know the old man spread the word she'd gone back to boarding school and everyone believed it—why wouldn't we?—but from the time that private investigator you hired told you she didn't—well, there had to be a reason for her to run away.'

'There could have been a dozen reasons for her to run away,' he told Belle, 'none of which would include pregnancy.'

None of which *he'd* ever been able to give credence to.

'Now, don't I have patients to see?' Flynn asked before Belle could start theorizing, not wanting to get any further into this conversation, which was already churning up the emotions he'd felt back then—anger at Majella for leaving as she had—for hurting her grandfather, a man Flynn revered. And for hurting Flynn himself in a way he hadn't been able to fully comprehend, although betrayal was the closest he could come to it. A betrayal of their friendship that had grown so slowly yet had seemed to have reached a new level just before she'd left.

He watched Belle stand up and walk towards the door. Had he sighed, that she turned and looked back at him?

'Are you OK?' she asked.

'I'll be better on Wednesday when the festival is over for another year,' he told her, to be rewarded with one of her array of 'women' looks—this one clearly saying, *Oh, you poor foolish man*!

'I wasn't talking about the festival,' she said, in case he hadn't read the look.

'I'm not sure that I was either,' he told her, then he waved his hand and she departed, already speaking bossily to the patients in the waiting room, organising them for him—organising them out of love...

Flynn got on with his day—lifting the phone to call the hospitals again, learning that bone fragments had been removed from Becky's brain, the chest wound had been closed, and she was now in an induced coma, while Patrick was stable after operations on his femur and lower legs and feet.

Satisfied that all was as well as could be

expected with his distant patients, Flynn moved on to those closer—mostly people like Belle who'd known him all his life; known his father, who'd walked out on the family when Flynn had been six; known his mother and naturally wanted all the latest news of her and the new life she was forging for herself with a man she'd met by chance last festival.

And if, as he worked, he wondered about the woman with the beads in her hair, it was only because his subconscious mind kept replaying scenes from the past—scenes he'd thought forgotten a long time ago.

CHAPTER TWO

Flynn!

Thoughts of him—memories—crept insistently around in Majella's head as she helped Helen and Sophie set up the Nature's Wonders stall. Behind them, in the area they'd set aside for a display on the Native Animal Rescue Service, Grace played happily with her toys.

She was such a placid child—Jeff's genetic legacy, for though Majella had practised docility throughout her childhood, she knew her own natural disposition was more volatile.

Jeff!

She closed her eyes and breathed deeply, dispelling the horrific pictures that invariably flashed through her mind when she thought of him. Surely a time would come when her first thought of Jeff would be of him alive—of the kind, protective teenager she'd first known, or the encouraging, supportive young man who'd stood beside her every step of the way through her tough army training, or even the gentle, loving husband—the father of Grace.

Shouldn't her memories of Jeff not be the pictures she'd seen of the fireball that had engulfed the crashed helicopter, killing not only him but other medical personnel going to the aid of storm-devastated people on a small island few Australians had ever heard of before the accident?

'Are you sure you don't want me to come with you?' Helen asked, her keen eyes scanning Majella's face—trying to read her mood.

'Do I look as if I need support?' Majella asked, keeping her voice light—making a joke of it. After all, what was the point of taking this first huge step towards personal independence if she needed Helen to hold her hand while she took it?

'You look haunted,' Helen said quietly. 'As haunted as you did when you first came to live with us.'

'One more injured animal to care for,' Majella remembered, then she hugged Helen, bent to kiss Grace, and walked swiftly out of the big marquee.

The real estate office was in a storefront—a shop Majella remembered as being empty and decrepit back when she'd left town.

'Mrs Sherwood,' the agent, a brisk-looking woman in her forties, greeted her. 'You're right on time. Now, as I explained to you on the phone, the property is a deceased estate and there are some clauses in the will which mean the executor of the estate likes to meet all potential buyers so he can explain the circumstances under which the auction might not go ahead.'

The woman paused, took a breath, and continued before Majella could question this statement.

'For this reason he usually shows buyers around the house himself. Unfortunately, he's not always as punctual as we'd like, but we'll drive out anyway—you can look at the grounds and outbuildings—and hope he's turned up by the time we're ready to do the house.'

She led Majella to a smart new four-wheel-drive, opening the passenger door for her, reciting all the time statistics about the town's growth and potential.

'We've five B and Bs in the town already but if that's what you decide to do with Parragulla

House, don't be put off—there's still a big demand for quality accommodation. And weddings—functions—it would be ideal for something like that.'

'Not a family?' Majella couldn't help asking. 'Is there something wrong with it as a family home?'

'Of course not!' The agent recovered quickly. 'It'd be ideal for a family, although…' strained laughter '…you look far too young to have a family.'

She was lying and Majella wondered why. Did an atmosphere of unhappiness haunt the old house? Did sad and lonely ghosts walk the verandas?

True, *she'd* been unhappy there, and possibly her mother had been equally unhappy as she'd grown older, to have run away as she had. But even as a child Majella had known it wasn't the house's fault. The house itself had been special, bright and spacious, yet full of secret nooks and shadowy corners, as if the potential for happiness was lurking there, just hidden from her sight.

'As I told you on the phone, the previous owner bred dogs—working dogs—kelpies—so there are kennels and runs behind the main building.' The agent's spiel continued. 'With the town growing so rapidly, a new owner could start boarding kennels, and the stables, although they're in poor repair at the moment, could be brought back into use. There are stalls for twelve horses. Do you ride? You could keep horses and start trail rides—they'd be popular.'

Did she look so impoverished the agent thought she'd need an income? Majella wondered. True, her pension and Jeff's insurance money hadn't made her wealthy, but she had enough, and this project wasn't about making money, but making a life for herself and Grace. Especially Grace. For how could Majella bring up a strong independent daughter if she hadn't first established her own strength and independence?

Tremors of what she told herself was excitement, not trepidation, ran down her spine as they drove beneath the high arch that hung above the cattle grid and up the long, tree-lined drive. The agent continued to chat, pointing out different outbuildings and fenced paddocks, but Majella had stopped listening, thinking instead of other times she'd been driven beneath the spreading trees—recognising the tremor now. Definitely trepidation.

Although today there would be no grandfather waiting at the top of the steps—her report card in one hand and his riding crop in the other—no need for trepidation…

But unless she was seeing things, someone was standing there—a tall, rangy figure in tan moleskins and a pale blue country-style shirt.

Grandfather's ghost?

'That track leads around the back to the garages and the dog runs.' The agent waved her hand towards the smaller side road. 'But I can see the executor is here—right on time—so I'll introduce you to him then let him show you through the house. I'll be waiting right here at the bottom of the steps, when you're ready to see more or go back to town.'

I'll wait with you, Majella felt like saying, but knowing this was the first small step towards the independence she sought, she opened the car door, and, with legs stubborn with reluctance, slid out of the high-set vehicle.

The agent was already climbing the steps, talking to the man at the top, but although Majella knew she should follow, she turned and looked back down the drive, towards the stables on the left, half-hidden by the trees. Then she swung around, knowing it couldn't possibly be her grandfather standing at the top of the steps, but hardly prepared for the man it proved to be.

'Dr Sinclair, this is Mrs Sherwood, the client who phoned about the house.'

The agent's introduction was succinct—so much so it echoed in Majella's head, over and over again, blocking her ability to think, or even make sense of the situation.

Her feet took the steps, one by one, with an achingly familiar heavy tread, until she reached the top.

'I'll take over now,' she heard Flynn say, then she felt his hand on her elbow, guiding her, steering her off the veranda, into the front hall— away from the agent.

'Are you all right? You're sheet white. Do you need to sit down?'

Did she look about to faint? What had happened to the strong independent woman?

Be practical!

'*You're* the executor of his will?' Though now she thought about it, she shouldn't be surprised. Her grandfather had always thought a lot of Flynn. 'What do executors do exactly?'

'Let's sit down.'

There was so much concern in his voice Majella forgot about being practical and looked at him—looked properly at him— seeing not the teenage Flynn she'd kissed in the stables that evening before she'd left but a man with blue eyes—worry in those sapphire depths right now—and soft black hair, tinged with grey already, and tiny laugh lines splaying out at each temple, white against his tanned skin.

Broad shoulders. He'd filled out since his teenage years, although he still moved with the easy grace of a horseman. Strong hands, tanned, nails neatly pared—images of Flynn...

Something fluttered in her chest, uncertainty and something else, and she whispered his name, talking to the man she saw, not the boy she re- membered, the wonder of it all echoing in the word.

'Oh, Flynn!' she repeated, lifting her hand to touch his cheek, not knowing what else to say— not knowing what to think or what to feel—not knowing anything.

After a moment that had lasted half a lifetime she moved away from him, into the living room, towards the window embrasure—one of the pleasant nooks she'd been remembering. *So much for strength and independence.*

Once seated—and away from his immediate presence—she could think again. Tell herself it was natural Grandfather had appointed Flynn as executor of his will, and that it didn't matter one jot. The house was up for auction, and it remained a house that suited her needs. More than that, it was the house she'd felt she had to see again—perhaps even buy, live in…

Flynn could still feel the imprint of her hand on his cheek although the touch had been softer than a feather's brush. Could still see her eyes— not the green of cats' eyes, or the emerald of lush grass, but the pale translucent green of streams fed by snow-melt in the mountains—a colour, yet not a colour.

He watched her move away, sit down; saw the sunlight catch the coloured beads plaited into her hair and heard the tinkle of tiny bells embedded in the braids. A stray sunbeam touched her cheek, gilding the skin, making the sprinkle of freckles across her neat, straight nose a darker shade of gold.

And something shifted in his heart.

'*Mrs* Sherwood?'

She spun to face him, making him realise he'd repeated her name aloud.

'Of course you'd be married. That's just wonderful,' he added lamely, although it didn't feel wonderful. But, then, he was still trying to come to terms with Majella being right here in front of him—still astonished by her presence, although he had known she was in town.

'And you?' she asked, her voice the same—slightly hesitant, as if uncertain anyone would ever want to hear her speak. 'Are you married, Flynn?'

No one else had ever said his name as Majella did. She breathed it softly, lifting it at the end so it always seemed a question. He stared at her—at the braids and beads, at the clear pale skin and sprinkling of freckles, at the woman's figure clad in jeans and a simple cotton shirt, covering curves that made his body unexpectedly stir—and his pulse beat a little faster.

She's married.

A twinge of anger prickled at his nerves—a weak and shadowy reminder of the hot emotion he'd felt at her departure, at her desertion of the old man. At least, that's what he assumed it was—the twinge.

'No!' he said, too loudly, making her frown as if she'd forgotten she'd asked a question. Then her face cleared and a teasing smile curled across her lips.

'You don't still believe that marriage is a sham, do you? Something invented by people selling dreams to gullible fools—wasn't that how you used to put it?'

She was changing the subject, he knew, but found himself defending his youthful cynicism.

'Given my father's track record, I had a right to think that way.'

She shook her head.

'No one could have taken better care of their family than you did, Flynn, so you can't possibly believe you'd follow in your father's footsteps.'

'Who knows? But my life isn't the issue here.' Irritated by the reminder of his brash young self, he spoke more abruptly than he'd intended, so his question, when he asked it, seemed to echo around the room.

'Where have you been?'

She frowned again, then she stood up and came towards him.

'Flynn, this is awkward, I know. I felt that at the accident last night. I wanted so much to talk to you then, but you were busy, and I had Grace in the car—Grace is my daughter—I couldn't stay. But we were friends once, can we not meet as friends again?'

'Friends? When you left without so much as a word of farewell? Oh, your grandfather explained—other friends, no doubt more important friends than a nobody in Parragulla—had returned to school early and you wanted to join them.'

Why was he repeating the old man's story when he now knew, from the investigator's enquiries, that the story was a lie?

Because, whatever the reason she'd left, he still blamed her—blamed her departure—for the old man's first debilitating stroke?

Or because of his own sense of hurt and betrayal?

Surely he'd got past that.

'He said that?' Majella whispered, stricken eyes meeting his, her obvious pain banishing his questions. 'Oh, the wicked man! I knew he wouldn't tell the truth, but I didn't know what tale he'd put about. I'm sorry, Flynn, but I had to go.'

'Had to go?' Flynn repeated, but she'd turned away again, returning to the seat beneath the bay window, kneeling on it this time, looking out at the rolling acres that stretched down towards the gate.

He waited, though for what he wasn't sure.

An explanation?

What would it mean after all this time?

Why did he care?

He watched her, seeing the way the thumb of her left hand toyed with the fine gold wedding band.

She was married…

That was good, surely…

Majella stared blindly out the window, knowing she could never tell Flynn the reason why she'd left.

He might be angry with her now, but Flynn had always had a basic decency and a strong sense of what was right. He would be horrified—devastated—if he knew what had occurred that night.

Thoughts and eyes came slowly into focus. She saw the car at the bottom of the front steps.

'The agent's waiting for me,' she reminded him, not turning back towards him. 'She said there's some clause that might put the auction in doubt. Is the house for sale?'

'It's actually yours,' Flynn told her, his lean face wiped clean of all emotion. 'You mentioned a daughter. The will was complicated—there were conditions—I'm sorry but I really don't have time to discuss all of them right now. But you've fulfilled the main ones—being married with a family…'

'Are you saying Grandfather left me the house, but only if I met some stupid conditions?'

Majella felt anger rage through her, and though it was directed at her Grandfather, it was fierce enough to burn away the Flynn-attraction she'd been feeling.

'They weren't that stupid.' Flynn defended the old man automatically. 'Considering how young you were when you left, he'd naturally have been concerned about you.'

'Pigs might fly!' Majella snapped.

'He changed, Majella. He had a stroke two weeks after you left, and though he recovered quite well from that one, he had several more over the years and became completely bedridden.'

'And I'm supposed to feel bad?' Majella demanded, although she did feel bad—guilt squeezing at her chest. Could he really have cared for her in his own cold way? Enough that her departure had caused a stroke?

'You're supposed to understand why he

included conditions,' Flynn said, his voice taking on the bossy tones he'd used to her through most of their childhood.

Bossy tones she'd longed to hear when she'd fled into that lonely night so long ago.

If only she'd had Flynn to tell her what to do, she'd thought. But that had been impossible…

But that had been then and this was now. Strength and independence, she reminded herself, and took a deep breath.

'And the conditions were?'

He studied her for a moment, then nodded his head as if conceding something in his mind.

'As I said, it seems you've met the most important one. Parragulla House was to be yours providing you were married and had a family or had started a family within twelve months of your grandfather's death. The actual date of this deadline is the first of October. I've been searching for you since he died—ads in papers asking for you or anyone who knew you to contact me or the solicitors, then a private—'

'I had to be married and have a family in order to inherit the house?' Majella's incredulous demand broke into what, to Flynn, had seemed a very straightforward explanation.

'Well, actually the condition states you have to be in a happy and stable marriage—those were the exact terms,' he explained.

'And just who was to be the judge of the happiness and stability of my marriage?' she asked, icily cool but once again a Majella he recognised. She'd been the most docile child he'd ever met, yet every now and then, especially if she'd felt some injustice had been done, usually to a dog, or one of the horses, she'd get angrier than anyone he'd ever known. Not a hot, yelling, tantrum-type anger, but a cold, determined anger that had conquered by its very coolness.

He hesitated, then reminded himself he was all grown up now and able to handle anything—including icy anger.

'Well, me,' he said, and heard his hesitation—not quite all grown up.

'Were you married when he appointed you to make the decision? Happily married? With your own family? Well qualified to judge happiness and stability in someone else's marriage?'

'I've told you I'm not married and I haven't ever been, but for heaven's sake, Majella, you're making too much of this. Do you think I wouldn't take your word you're happy? Can't you see your grandfather wrote the clause because he *wanted* you to be happy? Can't you understand that?'

'No I can't,' she snapped. 'All I can see is Grandfather's love of power. He always believed his word was law, and this condition is just his way of manipulating me from the grave. Well, I'm not bowing to his will or playing his stupid game. I assume he left orders as to what happens to the house if I don't fulfil his ridiculous conditions.'

'If you haven't inherited it within the twelve months, it's to be sold at auction—hence the ad that's been running in the papers for the auction on the eighth of October—we had to give people time to know about it. If that happens, the proceeds of the auction are to go to charity,' Flynn told her. 'But you're being stubbornly stupid about this, Majella. All I have to do is meet your husband, and having done that, I can't see why the property transfers can't go ahead.'

'My husband's dead and I'll buy the damned house—that's what I came here to do in the first place!'

And on that note she stormed out of the room, across the veranda and down the steps to where the agent waited in her car.

'Well, that went well!' Flynn muttered to himself, following more slowly, wondering how such tragic information as Majella's husband being dead could make him feel both sorry for her and, in some other way, relieved.

Majella walked swiftly away, proud of herself for not falling apart although her insides were as shaky as Grace's jelly moulds, and her nerves vibrated with a tension she'd never felt before.

Tension and anger!

The tension she could understand—just being near Flynn reminded her of her girlhood crush on him, and the foolish fantasies she'd dreamed as she'd grown up.

The anger was less easy to explain.

Was it anger at her Grandfather?

Or at Flynn for agreeing to be his mouthpiece?

Or at herself for caring?

She hadn't expected Grandfather to leave her the house so she knew the anger wasn't generated by disappointment.

She sighed, greeted the agent cheerfully enough and, as they drove away, asked how much she thought the house was worth.

'Because it's within the magic two-hour radius

of Melbourne—the distance people will drive for weekend escapes—and because it's such a pretty town, Parragulla has become very popular and prices have gone up accordingly. But I'd say if the auction reaches one and a half, the executor would be happy.'

'One and a half what?' Majella echoed weakly. This was Parragulla, a small country town.

'Million,' the agent said blithely. 'Maybe it could go as high as two, given the buildings and the variety of uses to which the place could be put.'

Majella leaned back against the leather upholstery of the agent's car, and sighed again.

At least now she understood why the agent was thinking in terms of her running a business. Anyone who bought the place would have to have a hefty income…

Flynn watched her leave, seeing the way her hips swayed as she moved, the graceful walk, not quite a glide, but silent, as if by passing quietly through life she'd not be noticed.

Not be noticed when the promise of her teenage beauty had blossomed with maturity? When, even with her cloud of dark hair restrained by beads and braids, she'd turn heads, male or female, wherever she went?

He walked slowly down the steps of the house that should, by rights, have been Majella's—without any ties or bribes.

His car was parked around the back—near the runs the old man had built for his dogs—and as Flynn climbed into the dirty, battered vehicle an image of a young Majella popped into his head. The small, slight girl standing in one of the runs, clasping a squirming kelpie pup to her chest, smiling in delight at its soft nuzzling. Then the old man appearing, frowning, his riding crop tapping against his leg.

'The dogs are not pets,' he'd told the child, who'd blanched and slipped the pup back into its pen, then scuttled away, up the steps, disappearing into the big house she'd shared with the old man.

Fearful?

Flynn drove away, away from memories. It was fanciful after all this time to think she'd paled at the rebuke, ridiculous to imagine fear in the way she'd fled. The old man had been strict, but he'd been the fairest man Flynn had ever met. Stern and unapproachable in many ways, demanding

perfection, yet fair in his judgement of the tasks
he'd set the boy who'd come to work for him—
the boy Flynn—and more than fair with his gene-
rosity, helping Flynn's family financially, putting
Flynn himself through university…

'I can't possibly afford to buy the house.'

Majella had returned to the stall and lifted
Grace into her arms, hugging her daughter close,
needing to feel her chubby warmth—needing
the present to blot out the past.

And with Grace still in her arms she'd turned
to Helen, wanting to see her friend's face as she
made this announcement.

'It was the executor you went to see. Who is
handling that job? Your grandfather's solicitor?
Or someone you know? Someone you might be
able to talk terms with?' Helen asked.

Majella gave a huff of sarcastic laughter.

'Talk terms with Flynn?' she muttered,
hugging Gracie even tighter.

'Flynn's the executor?' Helen echoed.

She was asking for a simple confirmation, but
Majella could sense a dozen other questions—
more emotional than practical—hiding behind it.

'He is,' Majella confirmed. 'It was—awkward.'
Helen nodded.

'Coming back was always going to be hard,
love,' she said, and she gave Majella and Grace
a quick hug then turned to tend a customer.

This was the first time the Sherwoods had ex-
hibited their natural products at the festival,
Majella remembering it from her childhood
and thinking it would be a good place to
promote their fledgling business. She and
Helen had discussed it at length, Majella
knowing a return to Parragulla—putting the
past behind her—was a necessary step in her
path towards the independence she sought.
Being part of the festival, she'd decided, might
be an easy way to do it.

So they'd booked a stall and then the ad for the
auction of Parragulla House had appeared in the
paper. Was the synchronicity of it an omen that she
was doing the right thing? Although she was far
too practical to believe in omens, it had felt right
to Majella—so much so she'd begun to consider
buying the old house, begun to see herself and
Grace living there, bringing life and laughter into
those secret nooks and shadowed corners.

* * *

Although the festival didn't officially open until the following day, today was for the locals, who wandered around the stalls, checking out new products and stocking up on things they'd tried before.

Flynn strode down the aisles. He might keep up his pretence of indifference as far as the festival itself was concerned, but he'd long since embraced solar power. Thanks to information he'd gleaned and equipment he'd purchased at previous festivals, he now had four eighty-watt panels on his roof, and this year he wanted advice on the inverters he'd need if he decided to put up more. And then there were the wind-farm people. He was pretty sure a couple of the new graceful windmills could provide enough stored power for the hospital in case of power outages and they could do away with the noisy generators they used now.

But today he had another object in checking out the stalls. The braided hair suggested Majella might be involved, combining her time at the festival with enquiries about the house.

Although the solicitors had told him over and over again that the condition of her inheriting the house was unbreakable, he knew there had to be a way out of this mess. And the best way to sort through it was to talk to her.

Talk properly, without emotion stirred by memories of the past intruding.

Was that the only reason he was looking out for her?

He felt the same stirring in his body he'd felt earlier and wondered…

As well as checking out the windmills, he wanted to buy some cakes of lemon myrtle soap for his mother. He'd been ten when he'd first walked past a stall and smelt the light, tangy fragrance. He'd bought a cake of the scented soap for his mother that year—with money earned riding the old man's horses—and had been buying it for her, on and off, ever since!

He glanced at all the stalls as he passed, then stopped to talk to a woman who now supplied the hospital with massage oil, which incorporated essence from the wild billy goat plum, known to natives in areas where it grew to be good for skin problems.

'The oil is wonderful,' he told her. 'We haven't had one person react negatively to it—even the most allergy-prone patients.'

The woman smiled her agreement—not an 'I

told you so' smile, but one of happiness that the product she'd developed and refined was doing good.

Flynn moved on, greeting friends and patients, lifting product samples and sniffing them, or rubbing cream into his hands. Not thinking of Majella. Well, not to the exclusion of all else. In the back of his mind was an idea that there had to be a more effective hand cream than the product they currently used at the hospital. Some of the nurses suffered dreadful irritations of the skin on their hands, brought on by the constant washing and drying.

He wandered back to the woman who sold the massage oil.

'No, I haven't anything, but there are some new exhibitors this year—a mother and daughter—Helen and Sophie Sherwood. They call their products Nature's Wonders. I know they have a hand cream and from what I've tried myself and heard from others, all their products are excellent. Very well researched, and completely natural.'

Sherwood?

How could he not think of Majella?

He continued in the direction the woman indicated, wondering whether they made a decent living, these people committed to providing the public with alternatives to the mass-produced and often chemically enhanced products available in supermarkets.

Wondered, too, about the Native Animal Rescue Service, whose big display he could see ahead of him. This was the first time he'd seen the service exhibiting at the festival, although he'd been reading a great deal about it lately. At first it had meant nothing more to him than occasional signs along the road, providing a phone number to call if one found an injured native animal, but now he knew there were sanctuaries springing up in rural areas, where injured animals and birds could be nursed back to health.

He drew closer to the sign, smiling to himself as he saw the image on the advertising poster— a small, pretty-face wallaby holding up a bandaged paw. Smiling even more broadly as a small girl wandered out from behind the sign, a tattered toy koala clutched in her arms—a living advertisement for saving wildlife.

Flynn squatted down in front of her.

'Is your koala hurt?' he asked, seeing the slightly grubby bandage around the koala's ear.

'Ear,' the little girl said, pointing at the koala's ear, then reaching for Flynn's, lifting her head as she did so—revealing clear pale eyes, the translucent green of rivers fed by snow-melt from the mountains.

'Gracie!'

A voice he knew, then Majella appeared from behind the sign, her hands full of bumper stickers that urged people to look out for wildlife on the roads.

'Man's ear!' the small child said, grabbing delightedly at Flynn's ear and tugging at it.

Majella dropped the stickers on the small table set up in front of the sign.

'You're with the animal rescue service?' Flynn said, detaching Grace's hand from his ear and offering her his fingers to grasp instead.

'It's why I went to see the house,' Majella said, her evident enthusiasm for the cause chasing away the coldness that had strained the air between them earlier, although some tension remained. 'The dog kennels and runs would be ideal recovery areas for injured animals, and with tourism growing in the region there are more cars on the road, so the service needs a sanctuary somewhere in this district.'

'We can work this out, Majella,' Flynn said. 'The house should have been yours without conditions—we can find a way through the legalities.'

She shook her head, such sadness in her eyes he wanted to take her in his arms and hold her until whatever pain she felt had passed.

Maybe kiss away the hurt...

Though he doubted a kiss would ease the pain of a dead husband...

He looked away, down at the child who was examining his hand and fingers as if they were novelties she'd not encountered before. She put her small palm against his far larger one and looked up at him, laughing in delight at the difference in their sizes—laughing in a way that made something catch in Flynn's heart.

Made something hurt!

Majella watched her daughter twisting Flynn's hand this way and that, examining his fingers—bending them and opening them again—intrigued as she always was by her ability to make things happen.

'I don't want Grandfather manipulating me,' she said, looking back at Flynn who ignored her statement, busy showing Grace how to lock her fingers together to make a church and steeple. His younger sister would have been Grace's age when their father had deserted them. Had Flynn taught her the rhyme? Opened up his hands to show her the people in the church?

And watching him with Grace, she wondered about the real reason why he hadn't married— hadn't had children of his own.

Because he'd already been a father to his sisters?

Had experienced more than his share of re-sponsibility?

Or because he feared he might be as irrespon-sible as his own father had proved to be?

Surely not—that was just too sad a thought to contemplate.

'Maybe it's not manipulation,' he said, settling onto the grass beside Grace and allowing her to clamber over him. So patient and caring towards a child he didn't know, so careful to make sure she didn't hurt herself. 'Maybe putting in the condition was a genuine attempt at reconcilia-tion. After all, you're the one who left.'

'I had to go,' she whispered.

'You said that before, that you *had* to go. Why, Majella? And what was so bad with your life that you never came back? The town found it easy to explain, writing your behaviour off as that of a spoilt girl, too busy playing with her city friends to bother with her stricken grandfather. Were they right? Was I wrong, thinking there was more to you than that?'

'No, Flynn, you weren't wrong,' she said softly, squatting beside him where he sat with Grace on his knee, once again touching his cheek. 'And thank you for not believing!'

Flynn looked down at the child, playing so trustingly with his hand.

Majella's child.

Her fatherless child.

He'd had personal experience of that often bleak condition and knew that children, whether boys or girls, needed a father…

One that stayed around…

'I'll talk to the solicitors again about the clause in the will,' he said. 'Surely once you've been married you've met the intention of the terms. I can't see that there's anything to stop you having the house.'

'Only myself—my own reservations about accepting it under such conditions,' Majella said sadly. 'I thought I'd buy it—that's what I really wanted to do—but when the agent mentioned the estimated price…'

She shrugged her disappointment, then glanced towards the stall where Helen and Sophie were busy with customers. 'I can't explain right now. Maybe I can't explain at all. At the moment, I should be helping over there. I was going to put out these stickers and lift Grace back behind her barrier. She's a little young to understand stranger danger and talks to everyone.'

She pointed to where a playpen had been set up, bright toys scattered on the grass, then lifted the little girl with her dark curls and pale eyes and placed her in amongst them.

'You're working on that stall?' Flynn asked. 'Sherwood's Nature's Wonders? Of course—your name is Sherwood. Your husband was related?'

Unsubtle way to find out about the man, Flynn realised, and immediately regretted it as Majella looked at him, eyes bleak and lips trembling slightly.

'He was Helen's son, and Sophie's brother,' she said softly. 'One split second of chaos and we all lost out!'

She walked away, crossing to where the other

two women were selling the products of their stall, smiling at a customer, reaching for a scarlet box and extracting a small bottle of essence from it, talking about its ingredients and use as if Flynn's careless question hadn't just cut deep into her heart.

'Some gynaecologists are now recommending casuarina—they're the trees we know as she-oaks—essence for hormonal imbalances and PMT,' she said, as Flynn watched and waited, intrigued in spite of himself. Were gynaecologists really recommending it, or was this just a selling ploy?

'They are!' a voice said, and he turned towards the older woman of the three, who, having completed a sale was now studying him with an interest that went beyond that of seller and customer.

'Do you read minds as well as selling essences?' he asked, and she smiled and shrugged her shoulders.

'No, but I know a sceptic when I see one.'

'Sceptic? Me? I'll have you know I'm well into alternative remedies whenever possible. In fact, I'm here in search of some hand cream I believe you've developed.'

'Not just to look at Majella?' the woman

queried softly, then she put out her hand. 'I'm Helen Sherwood, Majella's mother-in-law. You, I presume, are Flynn.'

Her presumption startled Flynn. It wasn't that he'd been Majella's boyfriend, but they'd been close enough for him to doubt she'd have talked about him once she'd married.

'Hand cream?' Helen prompted, and once again he had to set aside the muddle of past and present fusing to concentrate on the here and now.

He explained he was a doctor and told her about the skin irritations some of the hospital staff suffered from the constant hand-washing they had to do, and Helen turned away, returning with a good-sized yellow tube, a picture of a flower Flynn didn't recognise emblazoned on the side.

'It has a eucalypt oil base but with ti-tree oil and honey from native bees as well, which helps provide a protective coating to the skin so constant washing doesn't dry out all its natural oils. It's the loss of the skin's own protection that causes a lot of irritation.'

Flynn reached for his wallet but Helen waved away any offer of payment.

'Just take this tube and get the people who are most affected to try it. Then if it works, I'll make some up in commercial quantities for you which will be more economical than the tubes if you're going to use it throughout the hospital.'

He took the tube of cream then looked around the stall, trying not to watch Majella as she smiled at a young man with dreadful acne and pressed a small pot of salve into his hands, talking reassuringly all the time.

'There are some who say the essence of the dagger Hakea, Hakea Teritifolia, will overcome negative feelings or bitterness towards close family, friends and lovers,' Helen said softly. She lifted a tiny bottle from a stand at the back of the stall and tossed it to Flynn. 'A few drops in boiling water and inhale the steam, or just sprinkle it on your sheets and pillows.'

Flynn caught the bottle automatically, then stared at it, tempted to put it down on the counter and walk away, but Helen's smile was kind and he didn't want to hurt her by rejecting her gift.

Was it bitterness he felt towards Majella?

No way.

Negative feelings?

Maybe.

He walked away, glancing back towards her, and further back to where the little girl lay curled among her toys—the small hand she'd measured against his curled into a fist, the thumb fixed firmly in her mouth as she slept.

Majella's child.

Emotion, hard and hot, surged within him. It couldn't possibly be jealousy, although there'd been a time, in spite of his declared cynicism with regard to marriage, when he'd dreamed dreams where Majella's children would be his— dreams where they'd shared the house in which she'd lived, and filled it with kids and pets— filled it with all the love and laughter his family had shared. Even after his father had gone, not right away, but later, laughter had returned to echo through his family's house, and love had kept it warm and welcoming.

Young, and idealistic, in these dreams he'd seen himself making up to her for what seemed to him to be a bleak life of boarding school then holidays at home under the old man's strict regime.

While she—well, as far as he was able to fathom, she'd never seen him as other than a friend.

Until he'd kissed her…

And she'd run away…

CHAPTER THREE

THE alarm for the missing children was raised at ten the following morning. Two boys, aged four and six, last seen playing beside their parents' caravan in the showgrounds, disappearing in the few minutes it had taken their mother to walk from the van to the camp laundry only a hundred metres away.

'Well, look what the cat dragged in,' the local SES captain greeted Flynn when, summoned by the emergency siren, he turned up at the SES building which always served as a command post in any local crisis. 'All the woman did was go across to put a few more clothes into the washing machine. She started it and walked back, and by that time the boys were gone, vanished into thin air.'

Flynn was carrying his bag, not knowing when or even if it might be needed, but wanting it on hand. He rested it on a table as the captain continued to explain.

'Friends of the family have searched the camp site, but I imagine it was haphazard. There's some army woman here with the festival lot. She's out there organising a better search now—giving people grids to cover meticulously, including the area inside the show ring where the stalls are.'

Flynn knew exactly who the 'army woman' was, and felt an urge to join her searching group, so he could see the woman who'd once been so shy a girl giving orders to a diverse bunch of people.

But he knew in this kind of operation, everyone had a particular job.

'What can I do?'

'You *could* join in out there, as long as I can contact you if the boys are found and need attention. I'll give you one of the walkie-talkies. I've got one group down along the river, although it's unlikely they'd have got that far, and when I get another group together—it takes the country blokes longer to get here—I'll start them on the edges of the forest. I don't want to get too far ahead of ourselves when the kids could be hiding under a van somewhere, or in someone else's tent.'

Flynn left the building, which was situated on the far side of the showground, and as he walked past the stalls, still carrying his bag for it would have been senseless to leave it in the shed, he noticed that the business of the festival seemed to be continuing, although he did hear a loud-speaker repeating a message for everyone to keep their eyes out for two unaccompanied boys aged four and six, dressed in jeans and T-shirts and wearing, when last seen, cowboy hats.

But once past the marquees it was obvious a search was in progress, men and women moving in a line, getting down on their hands and knees to peer under caravans and cars, calling for keys to open van doors, car doors and boots, everyone tense and alert, a nervous energy tangible in the air.

'Jamie, Sam!' voices chorused, gruff voices and the high-pitched tones of teenage girls.

Flynn moved through them, seeking the search organiser, wondering about the mother of these missing children, and how she might be coping.

'Flynn!'

He turned to see Majella, squatting beside a folding chair, her arms around a distraught woman—obviously the mother he'd been concerned about! They were under a tented annexe attached to a large caravan.

'Would you happen to have a sedative? Naomi says she doesn't need one, and I'm not sure about sedation and pregnancy, but she's very distressed and it can't be good for the baby,' Majella explained. 'Naomi, this is Flynn Sinclair, he's the local doctor.'

Caring, practical and efficient all at once, Flynn realised as he took in Majella's explanation. All the awkwardness between them over the house and the will had been wiped away by fear for two lost boys and concern for their mother.

The woman, Naomi, had been sitting, bent forward with her head in her hands, and it was only Majella's mention of pregnancy that made him notice the bulge. The huge bulge!

Flynn knelt in front of the heavily pregnant woman who was hyperventilating now, breathing and crying at the same time, weeping for her sons, breathing for the unborn child.

'Your job is to keep this new baby safe,' he told her. 'We will find the boys.' He spoke so firmly and positively she forgot her tears, looking up at him with puffy, reddened eyes.

'You will?'

Hope fluttered in the words, a hope that squeezed dread within Flynn's chest. But she was not to know that.

'We *will*!' he repeated with so much conviction Naomi nodded acceptance and fished around in her big smock to find a handkerchief and wipe her face.

Then she heaved herself to her feet.

'I've got to go to the bathroom,' she said, and moved away, heading for the camp restrooms.

Majella stood up, thinking she'd accompany her, but the woman shook her head.

'I'm all right. I had to have that cry, but now I'm better. As the doctor said, I've got to be strong for all three of my children.'

Majella sank down into the abandoned chair and looked up at Flynn, who'd straightened as the woman had stood.

'Your words were better than any sedative,' she told him, hoping the turmoil she felt whenever she was in his presence wasn't obvious. Telling herself the turmoil was to do with the will, not Flynn himself. Telling herself lies. 'And no risk of harm to her or the new baby.'

She added the last bit so he'd know she was

thinking of the anxious woman not this new Flynn-Majella dynamic.

'Where are your searchers meeting up?'

Well, Flynn wasn't thinking of personal dynamics—and neither should he be with two children missing. He'd always had a strong sense of responsibility, and she'd seen it again in the way he'd spoken to Naomi, taking charge of assuring and reassuring her, being definite in his assurances, as if by saying it he could make it happen.

Which, being Flynn, he probably could.

'At the gate between the camping ground and the main showground!' she said. 'Then someone will come back to here to report, while the others go and join the teams going out from the SES shed.'

'You've done this kind of thing before?'

'Only once, a search for an old man who'd wondered from a nursing home near where I was based at the time, but I was also involved in post-earthquake rescue in southern Asia. There we had to search through every ruined building, under every fallen tree, always hoping to find someone still alive, although the bodies outnumbered the living people about one hundred to one.'

She paused, then, remembering, added, 'Of course, the bodies had to be found as well. Not only for sanitary reasons, but to bring peace of mind to all the loved ones they had left behind.'

'Southern Asia? After an earthquake? You've done that kind of work?'

She smiled at his amazement, although she could understand it. The girl he'd known had worried about getting dirt on a dress.

'It's what the army does best, that kind of thing, and, being in the medical corps, we were the first in, before the engineers and general troops.'

'But Grace is, what? Two? Three? Surely the earthquake…?'

'She's three and was nine months old when the unit went to Asia. I left her with Helen. I had to return to work.'

But although part of her mind was on the conversation—and busy blocking out the reason why she'd needed to work—most of it was on Naomi. Hadn't she been gone an unnecessarily long time? Majella stood up, thinking she'd better check.

Before she could move further, a loud cry pierced the air, then both she and Flynn were running, straight across the narrow access road and grassy play area, towards the restrooms.

'My waters! My waters broke!' Naomi whimpered, as Majella grabbed her shoulders to support her and Flynn hitched his arm around her waist from the other side.

'Come on, we'll get you back to the caravan,' Majella told her. 'Your waters breaking doesn't mean you'll have the baby immediately, but you will probably go into the early stages of labour and you need to be comfortable.'

'Do many of your soldiers have babies that you're so knowledgeable about childbirth?' Flynn asked, when they'd settled Naomi back in her chair in the annexe and he'd followed Majella into the caravan, where she'd gone to make their patient a cup of tea.

'I have had one myself!' Majella reminded him. 'And there are plenty of women in the army these days.' Then she grinned and added, 'Though I must admit I've never delivered an army baby. But we're trained for all emergencies—a bit like ambulance attendants with advanced resus and support skills, and I've done some obstetric work out in the field.'

She was stirring sugar into the cup of tea she'd

made—panacea for so many ills, strong sweet tea—but she nodded towards the segmented area of the big caravan where a section of a double bed was visible through partly closed concertina doors.

'I really wanted to check out the van. I didn't think Naomi would want to leave the camp in case the boys were found, and I wondered if we could deliver the baby here if we had to.'

'We?' Flynn repeated, feeling as if he was in a continual state of amazement as far as Majella was concerned. He'd got as far as realising Naomi wouldn't want to leave, but checking the van's suitability for childbirth? Majella was way ahead of him.

'You can deliver a baby just about anywhere,' he added, to cover his own lack of forethought.

'Don't I know it!' she said, making him feel amazed again—and possibly just a little bit inadequate.

This was Majella, the girl he'd taught to saddle horses, and how to keep the tack clean and lubricated with the use of saddle soap; how to lift a horse's hoof to check for damage; how to put polish on the hooves when her grandfather's horses had been going to the races.

He'd even taught her how to whistle with two fingers in her mouth, though he'd stopped the whistling business when he'd realised she'd been able to make a louder noise than he had.

Of course, she would have learned a lot in twelve years, especially in the army, but it just served to remind him how little he knew her now.

'She's having labour pains,' Majella reported, coming back into the van after delivering the cup of tea. 'Isn't there some concern about delivery after the waters have broken? Something about a dry birth?'

'She should be OK if labour's already started,' he said, then realised he should be tending the patient, not standing in the van thinking about Majella, or peevishness and especially not attraction. 'But I want to examine her and check the foetal heart rate so we've a baseline for the progress of the labour. Will she at least come inside?'

Majella went back outside, returning to tell him Naomi wanted to stay in the annexe, but would move to a couch they had there so Flynn could examine her properly.

'The hospital is just up the road and we could

leave word that's where you are,' he said, feeling he at least had to try to get the woman to a place where everything needed was on hand, should things go wrong.

'I don't do hospitals,' Naomi said firmly, as he listened to the steady, rapid beat of her unborn baby's heart. 'I see a midwife all the way through the pregnancy and usually have a midwife for the delivery. Or just Bill, it was, with Sam. Bill delivered him.'

She began to cry again, and Majella soothed her this time, assuring her they'd find the boys, telling her it was time to think about herself.

'About as useful as spitting on a bushfire, telling her that,' Majella whispered to Flynn, who was gently feeling the woman's bulging stomach, checking the position of the baby who was preparing to enter the world.

'It's coming head first,' he told the two women, 'so no worries there. Would you like a girl this time?'

More spitting on the bushfire but he wanted to keep Naomi focussed on her labour as much as he possibly could. There was also something called the 'Hawthorne' effect, a phenomenon where a woman in labour actually felt better when there was a professional on hand, soothing her and fussing over her. He wasn't certain he'd feel better being fussed over if he was in the pain women seemed to experience in child-birth—in fact, he suspected he might want to murder the fusser—but whatever worked was good as far as he was concerned.

Explaining what he was doing all the time, he snapped on gloves and knelt beside her, wanting to check the dilatation of her cervix and confirm the position of the head.

Third child, shorter labour, she was already six centimetres dilated, and the contractions were strong and although he hadn't been timing them precisely, he knew they were about five minutes apart.

'I want to walk,' Naomi said, 'or at least stand up.'

Majella and Flynn helped her to her feet but, although she got as far as the chair, another contraction gripped her before she could go any further.

'I'll sit on the ground,' she said, slumping between them so they had to lower her carefully onto the grass. Majella pushed the chair towards her, and Naomi rested her upper body against it.

'I've got to check the search teams,' Majella said quietly to Flynn, who nodded then watched her walk away. There was a dream-like aspect to this reunion with Majella—one of those dreams that are impossible yet during the dream seem quite normal, until you wake and remember you're not a rock star, nor would you ever be likely to be having break-fast with the Queen.

So watching her walk away was disconcerting. Would she come back or would he wake up?

Naomi groaned and shifted, but when Flynn suggested she might be more comfortable on the couch or in bed, she shook her head.

'Gravity helps, you know,' she told him when she could speak again. 'So does standing in the shower, but I guess I can't do that right here and now.'

He was pleased she'd made the little joke, because it meant the pain had diverted her thoughts from the boys, although they'd been missing so long now that anxiety was gnawing at *his* guts, so how much worse must she be feeling, beyond the barrier her pain had now created?

'If I squat, using the chair for support, it'll tip over,' Naomi said, struggling now to find a comfortable position. 'You could sit in it to keep it balanced.'

If I'm sitting in the chair for support, who catches the baby? And what am I doing, fussing around here, when I should be making preparations for its arrival.

'The couch won't tip over. I'll help you across to it and you can squat there. Are there baby clothes somewhere in the van? And a clean towel or sheet I can put down beneath you?'

He helped her to her feet but she was no sooner upright than Naomi gripped his arms again, breathing fast now, panting with the effort of containing her pain but not crying out at all.

'Cupboard just inside the door, got "Baby" marked on it.'

He found the bundle of linen in the cupboard marked Baby, and praised Naomi for being so well prepared. The bundle as far as linen was concerned, was not unlike the baby bundles at the hospital, and all of it was spotlessly clean.

'With the boys at the lively stage they are, I needed to be ahead of things,' Naomi told him, then tears streamed down her cheeks once more and all Flynn could do was hold her while she wept.

'We'll find the boys,' he kept repeating, but when his name was called on the emergency band of the two-way radio he moved out of the annexe, pretending he needed to be in open space to hear the message, but really wanting to be away from Naomi in case bad news came loudly through the receiver.

'No luck with the search parties in the camping area or the stalls, I'm sending three groups into the forest now. You know the forest behind the show-grounds as well as anyone—will you join the search but stay in contact in case you're needed?'

'Will do, but not right now,' Flynn said, then explained Naomi's predicament.

'Never rains but it pours,' the SES captain said, and Flynn smiled as he remembered the man's fondness for a cliché. Everyone in town—here we go again on small-town ways!—knew about it and teased him, but it didn't stop him using the well-worn phrases all the time.

Flynn returned to his patient who announced she was ready to push, and the second stage of delivery began, ending after only twelve minutes, when Flynn lifted a good-sized baby girl into view and handed her to her weeping mother.

For a moment he just stood and watched the pair, feeling the wonder and delight he always felt when he brought a new life into the world. Seeing the new miniature person breathing for the first time, peering around with puzzled eyes at a whole new world.

Had Grace's father seen her born?

Felt this wonder?

He closed his mind to the questions and turned his attention back to Naomi.

'You're sure you wouldn't like to go up to the hospital now?' he asked, as he realised just how little a doctor actually did at a delivery. The nurses kept up sips of water or provided ice blocks for the patient to suck. They did the soothing and the pillow fluffing, they monitored the foetal heartbeats and counted seconds between contraction peaks, and checked dilatation, then did the Agpar scores, weighed and measured the newborn, bathed and dressed it, cleaned up the mother and made sure she was comfortable. Now here he was, baby safely delivered, only a placenta to check but, instead of being able to walk away, he was it as far as support for the pair was concerned.

'I'm staying here. The van's our home. My husband is a wood-carver—he makes puzzles and pictures out of wood. I had both the boys in the van and planned to have this baby here anyway.'

Naomi was adamant. She had her smock hitched up and the baby nuzzling at her breast. He put one of the clean muslin clothes from the bundle across them both and found a plastic dish under the edge of the van. A dog's water bowl? Didn't matter, he could clean it out and use it for the placenta, and, after checking it and bagging it, he could get some warm water in the dish to sponge the baby and see to Naomi's comfort.

By the time Majella returned, he had the baby dressed—and felt an inordinate amount of pride in this achievement—and Naomi clean and fresh. She lay back on the lounge, the baby in her arms, the little crib Flynn had found beside the bed on the ground beside her so she could pop the baby into it if she felt tired.

But the way she clung to the baby, Flynn sensed it wouldn't leave her arms—no matter how exhausted she might be—until her boys were found.

'You didn't wait for me,' Majella protested, when she took in the scene in the annexe, and though anxiety was etched deep in Naomi's face she offered a weak smile as she showed the baby to Majella.

'There's no news, is there?' she asked quietly, and beads and bells jingled as Majella shook her head.

'But I spoke to a Mrs Jakes. She's coming back to sit with you. The doc here knows the forest like the back of his hand. He's more use in a search party than playing with the baby.'

Naomi grabbed at Flynn's hand.

'Go now!' she said. 'Go and find my boys.'

Majella watched Flynn's face as Naomi made her plea and saw both doubt and determination. He bent and kissed this woman he barely knew softly on the cheek.

'I'll find them,' he promised, then he straightened up and walked out of the annexe, leaving behind an air of such certainty that Naomi actually smiled.

That was the Flynn she'd loved, Majella realised. The one beneath the bossiness and know-it-all attitude. The one who'd say a thing, then do it, because that was his creed.

But finding lost boys?

Was it always possible to keep a promise—to make your assurances come true?

Majella didn't think so.

She checked the notes Flynn had left on the table, smiling to herself when she saw the kitchen scales beside them. Had he ever had to attend to all the details of a birth without a nurse or midwife on hand? she wondered. Somehow she doubted it, but he'd managed—as, she had no doubt, he always would.

Mrs Jakes came bustling in, preceded by the smell of fresh-baked cookies.

'I'll look after these two,' she announced, and Majella followed the path Flynn had taken, out of the annexe and along the service road towards the SES headquarters.

'Good,' the SES captain said as she walked in. 'I don't want to send Flynn out on his own, so you can go with him. He's taking a skinny gully on the edge of area three, probably too far away for the boys to have walked, but we need to check it and he knows the land down that way.'

'Shouldn't you be helping Helen on the stall,' Flynn asked—not exactly an expression of delight that she'd be his partner!

'She and Sophie can manage, and keep an eye on Grace at the same time. All the stallholders have cut back to a minimum of staff and have joined in the search. The problem's been finding enough locals to pair them with so they don't get lost and cause more chaos.'

As she spoke, Majella picked up a whistle from a range of equipment spread out on a table and slipped the lanyard attached to it over her head, then she took a water bottle and thrust it into the pocket of her jeans.

'Let's go!' she said to Flynn.

He didn't move, instead staring at her as if he couldn't quite believe she was real.

'Now!' she said, and walked towards the door, although it seemed to be several seconds before she heard his heavy tread following her.

'My car's here. I'll drive to where we have to start.'

He had a map in his hand, although she doubted he needed it—knew he didn't need it when, instead of turning onto the main road, he took the track that led along the back of the showgrounds towards Parragulla House.

'That gully?' she whispered, through suddenly parched lips.

Their friendship had been forged on horse-back, her grandfather wanting her to ride well and trusting her schooling in horsemanship to

Flynn. So together they'd ridden the trails that led into the forest at the back of her grandfather's property, stopping to drink from one of the trickling, tinkling creeks that fed the river. But the gully had been special, almost hidden, and they'd ridden it more often as they'd grown older, tying the horses by the tumbling creek, sitting a while on a thick carpet of wild violets, talking to each other about things other than surcingles and saddle shapes.

Talking about the way they'd change the world—no more hunger, no more fear, no more war—idealistic teenage talk, but heartfelt. Then later they'd talked about themselves, their own dreams, sharing little bits of themselves.

Tentative.

Shy.

Young!

'That gully,' he confirmed, skirting the property's eastern boundary and stopping behind the stables, once pristinely painted—white with green trim— but now a tired, dirty, dilapidated grey.

'Has someone looked in the stables?' she managed to ask, although her heart was beating erratically and nausea churned in her stomach.

It didn't make sense! The happiest times of her

childhood had been in the stables—with the horses—with Flynn.

Yet she was feeling far sicker now than she had when she'd entered the house. And feeling *far* more trepidation.

'We're to start there,' Flynn said, so emotionless she wanted to strike out at him, although he could hardly know her reaction—hardly know the kiss they'd shared right here—her first and oh-so-innocent kiss—had been the catalyst for her abrupt departure!

She followed him towards the fence, where he put his foot on the second strand of barbed wire, pushing it down, and held the top two strands up to make a gap wide enough for her to climb through. Then, in a movement as natural to her as breathing, although it had been twelve years since she'd held a fence for Flynn, she did the same for him, aware of the proximity of his body as he clambered through, aware with every cell of her body of Flynn the man, not the boy who'd been her friend…

They searched the stables in silence, Majella because a huge lump in her throat precluded speech. She wasn't sure if it was sadness, or something else, but no matter how hard she swallowed, it wouldn't go away.

'Majella?'

Had he noticed her distress that he came to stand beside her?

'Are you OK? Is it Grace? Does having a child of your own make you feel the boys' disappearance more deeply?'

He put an arm around her shoulders and drew her close, and though the sympathy he provided was for now not for the past, she absorbed it, letting it strengthen as well as comfort her, letting it steel her resolve to find the boys, a resolve he echoed with his quiet reassurance.

'We'll find them.'

She nodded against his shoulder then pulled herself free, checking the stalls, the tack room, neither of them speaking until they were once again in the open air, looking towards the hills and the start of the gully that was their search area.

'You take the right-hand side, I'll take the left,' he said, practical again, although she guessed the empathetic man who'd caught her mood wasn't far beneath the surface. 'Go about twenty paces out then back, so you zigzag up the hill. Don't go past the waterfall, it's too dangerous to climb alone—we'll go up together on one side then down on the other. You've got your whistle?'

She held up the whistle to show him it hadn't vanished since she'd hung it around her neck. Flynn looked at her for a long moment, seemed about to say something, then just nodded and began to walk, twenty paces from the creek, twenty paces back, calling to the boys, listening for replies, then calling again.

They reached the waterfall at the same time, Flynn stepping easily across the big smooth rocks to cross the splashing, gurgling stream.

'I'll lead,' he said, and, assuming her compliance, took off towards the bluff. Majella smiled to herself as she followed, but her smile faltered when Flynn reached back to take her hand, and the sensations that had vibrated through her in the stables returned, making breathing difficult and sensible thought impossible.

The bluff wasn't high but it was awkward, and climbing it required at least ninety per cent attention. But Flynn's hand was holding hers, as it had in dreams from time to time, and the rightness of it struck her even harder than the vibration effect.

'You've missed the foothold. Put your right foot into it then I'll haul you up to where you can grip this rock with your left hand. Come on, Majella, we haven't got all day!'

'Testy, testy!' she muttered at him, although maybe he was nagging because he, too, was feeling vibrations.

Iron-man Flynn feeling vibrations from clasped hands?

Hardly!

She shook her head but managed to grab at the rock with her left hand and with her right foot firmly anchored, heave herself up to the next small ledge.

'Kids would never have got up here,' she told him, when, panting with the exertion, she finally reached the top.

'I did it when I was six,' Flynn said, and something in his voice made her look at him. He was staring out towards the town, his face strained and his eyes bleak.

Not an iron man at all.

'Oh, Flynn,' she whispered, and now it was her turn to offer comfort. She put her arms around him, hugging not the man but the boy who, at six, had no longer had a father. He'd not only had to cope with his father walking out on them, to see his mother's grief and his sisters' bewilderment, but he'd then assumed the older man's role, feeling himself responsible for his mother and two younger sisters.

Flynn felt her body, soft and feminine, meld with his—felt his own respond—allowed himself five seconds—ten—then stepped away, muttering gruff thanks she might or might not have heard.

'I'll go thirty paces in then turn and walk parallel to the creek, you stay beside it, follow it to the next bluff, then we'll cross and go back down.'

No little boys in cowboy hats answered their calls...

CHAPTER FOUR

WEARY searchers thronged the SES headquarters, most clutching a fat sandwich in one fist and a steaming cup of tea or coffee in the other. Darkness had fallen, and where hope had once lifted the spirits and kept heavy legs moving, now despair curled in everyone's mind and weighted down the feet that still tramped through the bush.

'You've done enough,' Flynn told Majella, who had taken over the first-aid post in one corner of the shed.

'Do you think this is from a stinging nettle?' she asked, ignoring his remark but looking up from the leg of a man she was treating. 'Or an allergic reaction to some other plant?'

He knelt beside her to examine the leg, which had long red weals raised along the calf.

'Do you suffer from other allergies? Are there things that trigger asthma or hay fever or irritated eyes?' he asked the man, who was a stranger, not a local.

'Allergic to just about everything,' the man said. 'Stupid, really, when I like nothing better than being out in the bush.'

'Use an antihistamine cream,' Flynn told Majella, 'but if you get stinging nettle burn and the patient knows that's what it is, there's a new cream that's more effective for it.'

She spread antihistamine cream on the man's leg, then, as he left, with her admonishments to put on long trousers and a shirt with long sleeves if he wanted to continue searching, she turned and picked up a small purple jar.

'You mean this?' she said to Flynn, holding up a balm made from the sap of the cunjevoi plant, a big-leafed native of the lily family that often grew near stinging nettles. 'Helen Sherwood developed it, after using the sap from the leaves on nettle stings when she was a child.'

Another patient was approaching, a man with a bloody handkerchief tied around his leg, but Flynn had time to ask, 'How's Naomi?' before the man arrived.

Majella smiled.

'The baby is just gorgeous and Naomi's

holding up. Thanks for sending the nurse to see her. Mrs Jakes is kind but also talkative. The nurse insisted Naomi try to sleep and although she probably won't, she might doze a little if she knows the baby is all right and no one's talking at her.

'Yuck!' she added, as the new patient arrived and peeled off his handkerchief to reveal a bloody, lacerated leg. 'How on earth did you do this?'

'Missed my footing on a ledge and slid down about ten metres to the next ledge,' the man said, making Flynn wonder if it was such a good idea to have helpers from the festival in the search party.

But as the man sat down and Majella began to unlace his boots, Flynn squatted down to get a better look at the wound. The scrapes and scratches weren't deep, but they covered a large area. The man, he guessed, was in his sixties, healthy enough but at an age when wounds on the lower limbs could easily turn to ulcers.

'I'll clean it up,' he said to Majella. 'Can you check through that first-aid kit and see if there's some liquid skin—it's not really skin but a spray-on preparation that will cover the entire graze.'

'You'd cover it, not leave it open?'

It wasn't exactly an argument, but the Majella he had known had so rarely questioned his decisions he glanced up at her, saw the green eyes, not challenging but enquiring, as eager to learn as she had always been.

He explained his thoughts, wondering about her training, wanting to ask more of what she'd learned but knowing this wasn't the time.

Wanting to know so much…

It seemed to Flynn that they'd been patching people up for hours, but when he checked his watch it was only a little after ten. The next shift of searchers, including most of the patients he and Majella had seen, had gone back into the darkness, with torches now, while the police had called for trained dogs to be brought in. Every light in the showgrounds and the town had been turned on and a large fire burned brightly near the camping area, everyone hoping light might guide the footsteps of the two small boys.

Majella was leaning back in the chair they'd used for patients, sipping on a cup of tea, when she turned to Flynn, a frown marring the smooth skin of her forehead, her freckles standing out tonight against the tired paleness of her skin.

'I wonder if they found the cave?' she whispered, her voice indicating her uncertainty, and, it seemed to Flynn, an element of fear. Then she sat up, put down her cup, and said, 'Do you have a crowbar?'

The question was so urgent he answered without asking why.

'In the back of my car. I always carry one, just in case I need to move a tree or rock off one of the back roads.'

'A rock. We may need to move a rock. Come on.'

She headed out of the shed, not stopping to tell the organisers where she was going or why.

'What cave?' Flynn demanded, catching up with her as she strode towards where he'd parked the big four-wheel-drive. 'There are no caves around here.'

'There's a cave,' she said. 'Come on, get the crowbar and we'll walk. It's up that scree between the boundary of the showgrounds and Grandfather's property. It wouldn't have been far for the two boys to have walked.'

'There's no cave,' Flynn found himself repeating, although he half smiled at the awareness that this time it was Majella giving orders.

But a crowbar?

'It's got a tiny entrance. I used to go there when I was little but then I got too big to crawl through, but I always believed if I could shift the big rock near the front I could make the entry bigger.'

They were out of the showgrounds now, following a narrow lane that had once been used to bring the locals' milk cows in from the common, back in the days when every family had had a cow.

'Up here!' Majella said, scrambling as quickly as she could up the tumble of loose stones, well lit by moonlight. 'See that clump of bushes. The cave's behind them.'

Lumbering behind her with the heavy crowbar, dodging the stones and rocks she dislodged, Flynn indulged himself with disbelief. Hadn't he roamed these hills from childhood? Didn't he know every bush and stone and crack and crevice for miles around the town?

A cave? She was imagining it.

But now she was kneeling in the bushes, scrabbling at them, then her head disappeared and all he could see in the torchlight was a very shapely butt.

She was calling softly, saying the boys' names,

but so quietly he doubted anyone a yard away would hear them.

Then, as he once again squatted next to her, he heard her say, 'It's OK. We'll get you. You're all right. You're very brave boys. Very brave. I'm going to shine my torch inside so you can see the light. Do you think you could come close to where the light is?'

She backed out, face filthy but eyes gleaming with excitement.

'They're in there,' she said. 'Blow the whistle—no, don't blow it. The noise will echo in the cave and frighten them again. Damn, we should have brought a walkie-talkie, but we can't leave them now to go and tell someone. Break a branch off that bush and I'll push my torch through the opening. Once they have light, it won't seem so bad. And my water bottle, I'll push that through as well. I don't suppose you've got a chocolate bar. No, didn't think so, but I'll take your torch and put it on the ground inside the tunnel so I can see where I'm pushing things.'

She took the branch he broke off and disappeared again, talking softly all the time, telling the boys how good and brave they were, telling them to come and get the light and the water bottle and that soon they'd be out.

Flynn, meanwhile, was examining the rock formation. There *was* a rock that might conceivably be moved—if he were superman!

'They crawled in, can't they crawl out again?' he asked Majella, who'd emerged again, dirtier than ever. 'Moving that rock will be a Herculean task.'

'We have to do it so I can go in and help them out,' she said, so determined—so sure he could move rocks, and maybe mountains. 'The problem is, the entry tunnel is quite long, maybe six or seven feet, and from inside, although there's light from a fissure somewhere up the rock wall so the cave's not totally dark, the tunnel looks very dark—and scary! That's why they haven't crawled out.'

She smiled at him.

'So go to it, Hercules!' she challenged, but when he set the crowbar at the base of the rock, she stopped him, suggesting he move it more to one side, so they could use another rock as a fulcrum.

'Army training,' she said, as if his amazement had been spoken. 'We get to do all these totally useless exercises—or when we're doing them they seem totally useless—then, bingo, something happens, like this rock, and a long-ago memory of a yelling sergeant provides an answer to rock removal.'

She'd been setting up the rock she wanted as a fulcrum while she was explaining, then she joined him on the end of the crowbar and together, bodies working as one, they forced it down and down until Flynn was sure the solid steel would break, or they would both get hernias. Then a movement, only slight, and a groan of protest from the rock, but it *did* move, an inch, another inch, and then three or four, bringing a yelp of triumph from Majella before she remembered the echoes and slapped a hand across her mouth.

'Let me try now,' she said to Flynn, dropping to her knees again, calling to the boys, telling them about the signal Flynn would blow on the whistle to let people know they were found, and not to be frightened by it.

Flynn knelt beside her and saw the narrow tunnel she was preparing to squirm through, while voices in his head yelled in protest—telling him to stop her, it was dangerous, she'd kill herself.

'You can't go in there—you won't fit. Or the rock might move and you'll be trapped. There's got to be another way. Let me get some more help.'

She smiled again.

'While the boys spend more time frightened and alone? I don't think so, Flynn, and at least, if I get stuck, you'll know where to bring the searchers. But now the rock is moved, I will fit. The way it was, when I began to grow, my hips used to get stuck, although I'm sure there's a theory that if one's head will fit through an opening the rest of you should be able to.'

She bent to the small opening and called, 'I'm coming, boys. Jamie shine the torch into the tunnel, darling, so I can see.'

To Flynn's amazement, a light wavered in the darkness of the low cleft in the rocks and for the first time in this exercise he actually believed they'd found the boys. Oh, Majella had been certain, but what did he know of her these days? Hippy beads in her hair—for all her talk of army training he didn't actually *know* anything about her. She might have been chatting to leprechauns in the cave—might have been right off the planet.

He stood up and blew the three long blasts on the whistle to signal that the boys had been found.

Would anyone hear it and get word to Naomi and her family? The search parties had covered this area first and were now much further afield. The showground was close enough, but would people be listening?

He got his answer immediately—excited yells from the showground, then car horns sounding, repeating the three long blasts of his whistle.

Majella's feet had disappeared, but now he heard her voice calling to him.

'Flynn, Jamie's coming first. Can you lie on your stomach and push your hands as far in as you can so he can reach out to you as he gets into the narrow part? He can squiggle through but touching someone would be good.'

'Would be good' had to be the height of under-statement for a child who'd been trapped in a gloomy cave for more than twelve hours, Flynn realised as he lay full length and tried to squirm as far as he could into the narrow aperture, keeping his torch in front of him all the time so the child would see it and be reassured by the light.

A little figure appeared, crawling towards him,

one hand dragging a dirty cowboy hat containing a bundle of some kind.

'Hi, Jamie, I can see you,' Flynn said softly, not wanting to frighten the little boy with the echoes Majella had warned him of. 'You're nearly up to me. Can I take your bundle?'

'No, it's treasure and it's mine. Mine and Sam's. Sam cried a lot but I didn't, even with the bears.'

'You're very brave,' Flynn assured the child, but when the little hand reached out and clasped his, it clung on so tightly he wondered if Jamie's bravery had been all used up.

Holding the hand and talking all the time, Flynn wriggled backwards, until finally Jamie squeezed through the narrowest part of the tunnel and was free. Flynn folded his arms around the fragile body and held him tightly, telling him how brave he was, and that soon he'd be back home with mum and dad.

Jamie cried out his relief, clinging like a limpet, and though Flynn wanted to poke what he could of his big frame back into the tunnel to guide Majella and young Sam out, he couldn't let go of the child who was free.

'Hush, it's all right now. You're safe,' Flynn soothed, rocking the child in his arms.

Jamie snuffled a little more then moved his head, no doubt, Flynn realised, wiping his nose across Flynn's shirt.

'We heard bears out here, that's why we couldn't crawl back out. Bears roaring like bears do!' the child sobbed, and Flynn wondered if, by some cruel turn of fate, the echoes of the searchers' cries had actually kept the children in the cave.

'Sam's coming now,' Majella called, but though Jamie's storm of tears seemed to have passed, he still clung to Flynn's chest like a baby koala to its mother's back. 'I've wrapped him up so he's warm and toasty and I'm going to push him through like a little pretend train, going choo, choo, choo through the tunnel.'

Was the little boy so terrified he couldn't crawl?

Majella's tone was light, as if this was the best game in the world, but he sensed concern behind the gaiety.

Four was very young to be lost for so long…

'I've got to reach in for Sam,' Flynn told Jamie, then realised maybe Jamie needed to be involved. 'But we also need to keep blowing the whistle so people will know where we are. If I give you the whistle, can you do that?'

Jamie eased away from him and took the whistle Flynn held out to him.

'Blow three times as hard as you can then stop for a little while then three more and stop and keep doing it until you see people coming up the slope.'

Jamie nodded his agreement, but when Flynn disentangled the two of them and lay prone once again, he felt a small hand clamp around his ankle. Jamie wasn't going to lose himself again.

Flynn forced himself in until the narrowing refused to allow his shoulders to go further, and stretched out his hands, hearing Majella's soft choo-choo noises and the scrape of something on the rock.

'Choo, choo, choo. Choo, choo, choo. Nearly there, little Sam train, nearly at the end of the tunnel. And who's out there? Mummy and Daddy and a brand-new baby sister. Isn't that exciting? Isn't this fun?'

About as much fun as castration with no anaesthetic, Flynn thought, then the bundle reached his fingers and it was his turn to talk to Sam.

'Hey, little man, you're nearly out. Can you hear that loud noise? That's Jamie blowing the whistle to tell everyone the train's nearly at the station and the two lost boys are found.'

He got a purchase on the fabric Majella had wrapped around the little boy and began to pull him slowly over the rocky floor of the tunnel, talking all the time, until, moving backwards himself, he finally was able to hold the child in his arms.

Sam was wrapped like an Eskimo papoose, a solemn, tear-stained, grimy face wrapped in a motley collection of clothes and greying rags. And though he talked soothingly and Jamie chatted excitedly to his brother, Sam gazed at the outside world around him with fear-blank eyes.

'Look,' Jamie said, 'people coming. My whistle worked.'

And from down below people *were* coming, but before Flynn could celebrate he had to get Majella out of the cave and examine this child who had been through such trauma.

He unwrapped enough of the clothing to allow Sam to move his arms, but the boy lay still and limp. Flynn held water to his lips but it trickled down his chin, and the need to get him to the hospital became more apparent every second.

But to go and leave Majella in the cave?

He bent to the entrance.

'Where are you? Are you on your way out?'

he called, and though she answered, her words were distorted by the rock.

Or maybe tears?

Because the children had now been found? Women could cry from relief. Especially if they had a child of their own. And hadn't he got just a little choked up when he'd heard the voices and then lifted Jamie in his arms?

'Can you take off your shirt?'

Majella's voice again—still echoing or teary.

'Take off my shirt? Why?' he demanded, more of his mind on Sam whose pulse was thready, and whose vacant stare was really bothering Flynn.

'I wrapped my clothes around Sam. I need something to cover me when I get out.'

She was closer now, no echo, although her voice still sounded thick.

He put Sam down, grabbed Jamie who was about to plunge headlong down the scree to greet a man who apparently was his father, and managed to take off his shirt while keeping one hand on the two children all the time.

'You found them!'

The man who'd rushed ahead scooped his elder son into his arms then reached down for Sam. But when the little arms didn't reach for him as Jamie's had, the man dropped to his knees and gently lifted the still bundled child up against his chest.

'It's OK, Sam, boy,' he whispered. 'Daddy's here now. You're safe.'

The man's voice was cracking, Flynn was swallowing hard, then a scrabbling noise behind him reminded him the heroine of the exercise was yet to emerge.

She crawled out, the moonlight showing a filthy, blood-streaked woman, clad only in a bra and skimpy pair of panties, clutching a small cowboy hat in her hands. Flynn wrapped his shirt around her, pulling her into a hug at the same time, then, while his head wanted to yell at her for putting herself at such risk and his heart wanted to hold her for a bit longer—a lot longer—he went into responsible mode and began to give orders.

'I'll take Majella back to the hospital and I want you—' he turned to the boys' father '…to bring both boys up to the hospital so I can check them out.'

No need to worry him by saying it was Sam he really wanted to see.

He remembered the family logistics and added, 'Naomi won't want to be separated from them so soon after they've been found, so bring her and the baby as well. You can continue your family reunion just as easily there.'

The man looked from excited Jamie, whooping by his side, his bundle of treasure still clutched in his hand, to the silent child he held in his arms. He nodded to Flynn as if he understood.

'I'll bring them all straight up,' he said.

The man took off down the hill, followed by the other relieved searchers eager to spread the word that the whistle's signal had been correct and both boys had been found.

Flynn turned back to Majella, who was trying to get a shaking arm into the sleeve of his shirt.

'Hey,' he said gently, taking her hand and guiding it into the sleeve then wrapping his arms around her again, holding her close, pressing kisses on her hair, her dirty cheek—her lips.

Heat flared through his body, so unexpected he forgot to breathe, kissing her more deeply now, feeling her response, as hot and desperate as his own, aware in some far corner of his mind that this was utterly and absolutely both the wrong time and the wrong place, yet unable to stop.

'Flynn.'

His name, muffled by his lips on hers, broke the spell, and he turned, kept an arm around her shoulders and led her down the scree, steadying her when loose stones rolled beneath her feet, holding her because he couldn't let her go, didn't want to let her go—ever.

Where had that thought come from? The 'ever' thing? The kiss he could put down to relief that she was safe, and the boys found, and, if he was honest, to the attraction he'd been feeling towards this adult Majella ever since he'd met her.

But he'd been attracted to many women over the years, without ever considering an 'ever' as in not wanting to let them go—

'Our cabin's just along here. I'll be OK now. Thanks for the shirt,' she said, detaching herself from his side when they reached the bottom of the hill and the caravans in the showground were only a hundred yards away. 'I'll wash it and get it back to you.'

He stared at her in disbelief, then realised she hadn't been party to his thoughts.

Though she'd responded to his kiss…

'You can't just walk away,' he said, searching hurriedly through his bemused brain for a valid reason to keep her close. 'Apart from anything else, you've cuts and scrapes all over you. I need to look at them, treat them, patch you up a bit.'

She half smiled and shook her head.

'I can patch myself up. Done it dozens of times. Or Helen and Sophie can do it. I really need to get back to the cabin now, Flynn. Apart from anything else, I need to check on Grace, need to see her. Also, with the festival closed for the night, Helen will be getting anxious.'

'Then we'll call by the cabin, you check on Grace and tell Helen where you'll be, *then* we'll go to the hospital.'

She shook her head, and though Flynn was desperate to have her with him—he'd think more about *that* later—he couldn't find a way to make her bend to his will. She was no longer the Majella for whom his word was law.

He remembered the blank eyes of the child.

'I'd like you to come for Sam,' he said. 'He seems to have gone into cataplexy. You're the one he saw first, maybe you can break through.'

'Even when his parents can't?' she asked, but he sensed her wavering and nodded.

'OK. But I'll shower here, dab some antiseptic on my scrapes, and put some clothes on first,' she told him. 'Then drive up. I won't be far behind you, and you'll have to examine both him and Jamie.'

He had to accept this was as close to agreement as he would get, so he touched her on the shoulder and moved away, trying not to think of the long legs that had stretched below the hem of his shirt or the streak of blood that crossed the scar beside her eye.

Trying not to think of the kiss, although the legs had made his pulse beat faster and his blood heat again.

But the blood on the scar had somehow hurt his heart.

He arrived at the hospital just as the family pulled up. Naomi must have taken one look at Sam and seen the need for haste. She climbed out of the front seat of the big vehicle, the little boy in her arms, still swaddled in Majella's garments, although a bright yellow bunny rug with red chickens on it had been wrapped around him as well.

'What's wrong with him?' she whispered to Flynn as he got out of his car.

'I think it's just shock—and remember he'll be dehydrated as well. I want to get fluid into him fast, then take some blood so we can see if there's anything chemically wrong.'

He hated the idea of prodding and probing the little boy and sticking needles into him, but fluid resuscitation was a must so needles there would have to be.

The boys' father, now introduced as Mike, carried Jamie on his right hip, and the baby capsule in his left hand, and so the procession wound into the hospital, Flynn leading the way to the fortunately deserted A and E.

With Naomi's help and a constant stream of cheerful chat to her younger son, they unwound the clothes from Sam's small body. Talking all the time to the little boy, and with Jamie watching closely and telling Sam all over again what was going on, Flynn found a vein in the back of Sam's left hand, withdrew some blood for testing, then taped the cannula into place and started a drip.

The examination began—the usual checks of blood pressure, pulse, respiration rate and temperature, nothing to get alarmed about, nothing to explain the child's flaccid body and lack of response, even to his parents.

Physical examination next. Both knees were

scraped, but though Flynn examined every inch of skin, wondering if a spider bite or insect sting might be the cause of Sam's inertia, he could find no puncture marks or redness indicative of a bite.

'You're safe now. Talk to Mummy,' Naomi begged but the little lips stayed closed, and the brown eyes, like his mother's, remained fixed on some point on the ceiling.

'It's shock,' Flynn told Naomi, urging her into a chair beside the examination table. 'He'll come out of it.'

Naomi offered him a strained smile.

'You said you'd find the boys and you did, so I suppose I should believe you about this,' she whispered, and Flynn, though far less sure about the child than he'd been about the outcome of the search, nodded his acceptance of her faith.

He tucked the bright blanket around the little boy. It was obviously a favourite, then turned as Jamie announced he was going to show Sam the treasure.

'This will make him better,' Jamie said, dumping the dirty bundle he'd been carrying on the edge of the bed and peeling away the wrapping, which appeared, from its faded stripes, to be an ancient teatowel.

Inside was a small rag doll, gnawed by some rodent that had no doubt dwelt in the cave, and some pieces of metallic paper, brightly patterned, like the covering of chocolate Easter eggs, two marbles and some dull coins, one dollar and two dollar, while a silver bracelet with a broken catch completed the trove.

'Look, Sam, at what the fairies left behind when they moved out of our cave,' Jamie said, holding up each item one by one, his stubby fingers, still grubby from his adventure, smoothing the silver paper carefully.

Sam responded to the extent his eyes moved as Jamie waved each piece of treasure in front of him, and when Jamie added, 'And the fairies got us out, didn't they? I told you they would,' Sam's eyes closed voluntarily for the first time since Flynn had pulled him free.

'Sleeping?' Naomi whispered hopefully, and Flynn didn't like to disillusion her, although if Sam had closed his eyes in order to avoid looking at reminders of his ordeal, that, too, was good.

He checked Sam's pulse then stood up, intending to leave the family together while he tested

Sam's blood sample, but as he turned to leave, Majella walked in, clad in a long floaty dress that frothed around her calves and hid, yet in some way still revealed, the curves he kept on noticing. The beads were gone, and her hair, released from the tortuous braids, had reacted by flying every which way. She lifted her hand to it and smiled ruefully.

'It was full of spider webs and probably bat excreta—I had to take it out.' Then she moved closer, and he saw her eyes take in the dirty teatowel and Jamie's little pile of treasure. Every vestige of colour left her face, and with a sigh she collapsed onto the ground in a dead faint.

CHAPTER FIVE

HE LEFT his other patient, moving to the fallen woman in two long strides, but she was already stirring by the time he reached her, struggling to sit, apologising for being stupid, pushing him away.

'Lie still,' he ordered, and sliding one arm under her legs, the other under her shoulders, and lifting her as if she weighed no more than Sam. 'Stay with Sam,' he told the flustered nurse who'd followed him then gone ahead to open the door into one of the cubicles that ran down the centre of the A and E. 'Keep his family talking to him. I'll check Majella out and be right back.'

'Majella?' the nurse repeated. 'Majella Goldsworth?'

She was peering at Majella's face as Flynn laid his burden gently on the examination table, but none of the locals had known Majella well, her public appearances having been limited to church attendance by her grandfather's side, and that only during the school holidays.

He shut the door of the cubicle and turned to the woman who was causing so much internal chaos in his life.

'Are you pregnant?' he demanded, and she had the hide to the smile.

'Not unless it's a virgin birth, Flynn,' she said, sitting up and swinging her legs, slightly shakily, off the table. 'Well, not quite virgin, but Jeff died three years ago.'

Three years ago? And little Grace was three? Had the child never known her father?

'I'm sorry about fainting like that,' she continued, while he tried to control his racing suppositions. 'I'm generally not a fainting person. Reaction to seeing little Sam in the light, I suppose. He's not well, is he?'

She made to stand up but he grabbed her shoulder and forced her back down.

'No he's not, but you won't divert me that way. People don't faint for no reason. Let me look at you.'

Panicky green eyes caught and held his.

'I checked myself all over, Flynn,' she whispered. 'Truly, there's nothing wrong, but you're right, it wasn't seeing Sam. It was seeing those scraps of rubbish Jamie called his treasure. I don't know why, but it took me back—back to when I used the cave as a kind of little house all of my own. I thought the silver paper was precious—I saved it there...'

'Why?' Some inexplicable emotion had thickened his throat, surely not the thought of a little girl—Jamie's size—crawling in and out of that dark tunnel. Even as an older child she'd been scared of snakes and spiders so what impetus would have been strong enough to force her into that darkness?

'It was my secret place—a special place. I used to take my clothes off, you know,' she said, not answering him at all, diverting him, he suspected,' and put them in a plastic bag so they wouldn't get dirty, and I'd tie an old teatowel around my hair to keep the spiders out.'

She half smiled at the memory, but although it *was* a smile, Flynn once again felt a movement in his chest—his darned heart, tugging at strings that he knew, anatomically, didn't exist.

'Go back to Sam, I'm fine,' Majella told him. 'Fainting like that was silly. Hunger would have contributed. I should have eaten one of those sandwiches earlier.'

Flynn hesitated, but the faint had been real, no matter what the cause.

'First I'm going to examine you,' he said. 'Blood pressure and pulse at the very least. You mentioned bats—you could have an open wound somewhere that's got infected and no matter how good you are at treating yourself, you can't do all the areas of your back.'

She stiffened as he touched her—the slightest flinch, but enough to remind him of the tremors that had shafted through him when he'd kissed her. There were ethical considerations here. Ethical considerations when all they'd shared had been a brief hot kiss? Two kisses, if you counted the one they'd shared as teenagers.

Maybe not an ethical consideration, but he remembered the tremors, the heat, the shifting in his chest—

'You've got a patient waiting out there,' Majella repeated, interrupting his thoughts. 'Little Sam needs you more than I do. What's wrong with him, Flynn? Some kind of catatonic shock?'

He stared at her, this woman whom he knew

but didn't know, asking about the child. He switched his own focus back to Sam.

'I don't know enough psychology to be able to say, but I've a friend in Melbourne, a paediatric psychologist, who will be able to help. Actually, I think part of it could be physical—he was badly dehydrated and in such a small body that's a dangerous situation. I'm hoping that's the case, and that with fluid replacement and his family around he'll soon realise he's safe and the trauma is over.'

Majella nodded, pleased she'd diverted Flynn from talk of an examination.

'Maybe the baby will interest him,' she suggested, and although Flynn gave her a strange look, he did leave the cubicle, telling her he'd send a nurse to take her blood pressure and check her wounds, no matter how superficial she thought them.

The nurse duly appeared, checked Majella's blood pressure and pulse, dabbing ointment on some scratches on her arms, covering a cut with a small plaster, talking all the time about how wonderful it was the boys had been found, although behind the chat Majella could hear the questions the young woman wasn't asking— questions about Majella's return to town.

'Now rest a while,' the nurse said, as she carried the debris from swabs and dressings out of the cubicle.

But Majella had no intention of resting there, or of having further contact with Flynn that evening—or, if she could help it, for the rest of the weekend. For a start, it would be too easy to fall back into the habit of his company, and the warmth and comfort she'd always found in it. Not good thinking for a woman bent on finding independence.

Added to that was a second problem. Just the little she had seen of him had reawoken all the longings in her heart, so while her bruises might ache and her scratches prickle painfully, the bit of her that really hurt was centred in her chest!

And then there was the kiss. So inappropriate, to be kissing Flynn when the little boys had just been found. A kiss of celebration that they were both OK might have bordered on acceptable, and that was undoubtedly why Flynn had kissed her. But Majella's body had found the kiss much more than celebratory. In fact, just thinking about it brought back the hot, shivery feeling she'd experienced when Flynn's lips had pressed against her braided hair, her grubby skin—her mouth…

Perhaps she *should* rest a while.

Inside her head she heard a scoffing laugh and a reminder that the sooner she left the hospital the better off she'd be.

Naomi was holding the baby close to Sam when Majella, feeling acutely embarrassed by her earlier collapse, emerged from the cubicle. No change to Sam's expression, until the baby gave a cry and the little boy sat up and looked at his tiny sister.

'She's crying,' he said, and everyone in the room let out a cheer—no doubt the wrong thing to do as young Sam started at the noise then he, too, began to cry.

Naomi passed the baby to Mike and lifted Sam into her arms, hugging him and crooning to him, telling him how loved he was, how brave, how wonderful. Flynn was helping Jamie wrap his treasure, talking all the while to him so he didn't feel left out of the family celebration.

He's a good man, Majella thought as she watched the scene play itself out. She was about to leave when the nurse she'd seen earlier appeared, carrying a tray with a teapot, cup and saucer, and a plate of sandwiches on it.

'Flynn said not to let you leave until you'd eaten,'

she said, and Majella, suddenly so hungry she knew she wouldn't refuse, took the tray back into the cubicle, not wanting to intrude on the family.

She sat down on the couch, with the tray beside her, and devoured the sandwiches between sips of tea, then, replete, she rested her head back against the wall and dozed for a few moments, knowing she should go back to the showground, check on Grace and get some proper sleep.

Flynn woke her with a light touch on her shoulder, startling her for an instant, then, as she came out of her dreamy state, it seemed so right that it should be Flynn, she smiled at him.

'Are you OK?'

His voice was as gentle as the knuckles he brushed across her cheek, and she caught his hand and pressed a brief thank-you kiss against it before nodding her reply.

'And Sam?' she asked.

Flynn smiled at her, causing tremors that were so unexpected—so unlike anything she'd ever felt before—she wondered if she might be ill. Heat seared through her body, and she knew it must be flooding colour into her cheeks, but she was powerless against it—against whatever it was that smile had generated.

'Come and see,' he said, and it took a moment to remember she'd asked a question and another to remember what it had been. She stood up and Flynn slipped an arm around her waist—to guide her, nothing more, although the heat fired up again, making her knees unreliable and her lungs choke for air.

Pull yourself together!

It was an order she'd given to herself often over the years, and before this, it had usually had *some* effect.

Not tonight! Not on a betraying body that wanted to lean into Flynn's casually supporting arm, to turn within it so her breast rested against his chest!

Was it because she was still half-asleep that these thoughts and feelings bombarded her?

Weakened her?

She straightened up and shook her head, moving away from that unwittingly seductive arm, telling herself it was exhaustion making her body feel hot and shaky. Reminding herself she was a responsible adult—the mother of a child—not some teenage virgin trembling at the touch of an adored pop idol. For only so could she explain her extreme reaction...

The unknowing cause of her body's peculiar

behaviour led her back along a corridor towards the front foyer, then knocked and opened a door on the right. Inside, Majella saw a double bed, a folding bed and a small crib. Jamie was already asleep in the folding bed, while Sam and the baby lay between Mike and Naomi in the double bed. As Majella watched, Sam carefully tucked the bright chicken blanket around the baby and said goodnight to her, then snuggled up against his mother.

'This is our family room,' Flynn said, such pride in his voice Majella knew it was his innovation.

'It's wonderful,' she said, as she waved goodnight to the family and withdrew. 'For all your teenage talk of travelling the world, you were obviously meant to be a country doctor. You understand the people and their needs. You personalise medicine in a way you never could in a big anonymous city practice or major teaching hospital.'

She was surprised to see a faint flush of embarrassment colour his cheeks.

'It's not all good,' he said quietly. 'In the country you know the family so you get used to thinking of them as a whole unit, not little separate bits, but there are so many limits in country practice it's easy to get frustrated. And if you're not careful you can get bogged down in this family welfare stuff when you could be doing more preventative medicine and more study on new techniques and drugs. I need to know more, learn more, Majella, before I can be sure I'm giving my patients the very best service available.'

They'd walked out through the foyer and down the shallow steps while Flynn had been speaking, and now stood beneath the spreading pepper tree that sheltered a small lawn in the centre of the circular drive in front of the hospital. It was after midnight but the moon was full, the festival dates set around the full moon every year. The clear silver light it shed made the sleeping town look like something out of a fairy-tale.

Behind it, the high, forested ranges reared like ramparts, while the narrow river curling around the town could be a moat.

'It's beautiful,' she said, nodding at the scene spread out before them, more in affirmation to herself than conversation.

'It always has been,' he said quietly and she

knew they were back at the conversation they'd had before.

'I had to go,' she said yet again.

'So you keep on telling me.' He put his arm around her and tucked her up against his body. 'Yet you've come back. You came to buy the house. Why?'

Majella hesitated, then realised that explaining why she wanted the house might help to clear up some of the muddle in her own mind. She moved away from Flynn's protective arm so she could put her thoughts into words without distraction. 'I want somewhere for myself and Grace—a place of our own. Somewhere I can begin to build a life for us.'

She paused, seeking to explain a concept that was only vaguely formed within her mind.

'It's hard, because Helen doesn't really understand, and in doing this I know I'm hurting her, and she's the last person in the world I should be hurting. She took me in, you know. There was an injured koala and Helen picked it up for the animal rescue service—and took me as well. So from then on, there was always a Sherwood to take care of me—watch over me, Helen, or Jeff, or Sophie—so generous with their love and support I understood for the first time what a family was all about. And now there's Gracie, and they adore her, too, and in a little way she helps them accept the pain of their loss, but…'

Flynn heard the explanation, but his head was following the wrong threads, first the one about the rescue service—he'd passed the signs thousands of times and had wondered if anyone ever rang the number.

Then with the mention of Jeff his thoughts switched to the man Majella had married, wondering if the bloke had taken unfair advantage of her vulnerability and innocence, seducing her with ease within this new delightful thing she'd found—a family!

He didn't grind his teeth, although it was a close call—remembering just in time a couple of expensive crowns he'd recently had done. Majella was still talking, something about having to learn to stand on her own two feet— to be strong and independent for herself, but even more importantly, for Grace.

Then she turned towards him, expectant, no doubt waiting for him to approve whatever it was she'd been saying, but any words he might have said were lost when he saw her face lifted to his—skin pale and luminous as a perfect pearl in the silvery moonlight—features haloed by the dark hair.

A fiercely strong wave of emotion washed through him, weakening his muscles to the extent he reached out to hold her shoulder for support.

'*You're* beautiful,' he said, repeating the word she'd used about the town.

She shook her head as if to deny the compliment, but beneath his hand he felt her tremble, and as he drew her into his arms she shivered, although her skin was warm enough to suggest it wasn't from the cold.

She had strayed beneath the tree as she'd explained her need for independence, pulling at the long trailing branches, twisting them as she'd talked, so now they fell about them, making a cave of privacy.

Was it the shadowy darkness that made Flynn's blood thicken as she melted against him, made his pulse race when his lips met hers?

She met his kiss with a heat as unexpected as it was erotic, her tongue tangling with his when he thrust it into the warm sweetness of her mouth. His hands, resting lightly against her shoulder blades, felt the quiver that ran through her body, and that, more than the taste of her mouth or the feel of her full breasts nuzzling against his shirt, made him pull her closer, clamping her hard against his body so he felt the softness of her against his chest, his hips, his thighs.

Fierce desire coursed through him, blanking out his mind, concentrating all his being on the physical delights of touching her, holding her, feeling her skin and flesh and bones, the scent of her filling his nostrils, hunger for her vibrating through his body.

'Flynn.'

His name fluttered off her lips and onto his, but he wasn't ready to release her yet—to stop this kiss that had shifted his world off its axis.

'I need to breathe.'

The whispered words penetrated the fog in his head and, moving so he could tilt her head and see her face, he looked at her, skin dappled by the moonlight through the leaves, eyes beautiful and trusting, reflecting a little of the wonderment he himself was feeling. Then he bent his head and claimed her lips again, letting her feel the heat stirring in his body and the burning excitement racing along his nerves.

Majella felt his lips move on hers, testing and exploring. Felt her own response in a sudden rush of warmth deep inside her body and a melting sensation in her bones. She kissed him back, as much in the spirit of exploration—how much better could her own sensations get?—as for the kiss itself, then her thinking became blurry as Flynn's hands brushed against her skin. Now his fingers tangled in her hair, holding her more firmly, pressing her body against his, so she could feel his response as well as her own.

Kissing.

She'd never put much thought to it—could barely remember her reaction to Jeff's gentle kisses—but now, as Flynn urged her deeper into the shadows of the tree, she discovered a kiss could turn her blood to liquid fire and make her whimper with what she presumed was need, especially when his hand moved against her breast, outside clothes and bra but still generating fiery trails of longing that made her move against him, seeking some relief.

'Come back to my place,' he murmured, the movement of his lips felt on her own, and though she nodded, the thought of getting naked in front of Flynn, being naked with him, made her stiffen.

And it cleared her mind so although she kept on kissing him, not wanting to lose the feel of his lips on hers or the special closeness of his body, her thoughts turned to practical matters.

What was she thinking?

The issue wasn't getting naked with Flynn— nor even going back to his place. She was a mature woman—with a daughter, respon- sibilities. She was here to find out if Parragulla might provide the home she sought—her own home—not to get entangled with a man.

She eased her body just far enough away from his to break the sedulous attraction of the kiss.

'No, no, I've got to go,' she said lamely. 'Thank you.'

She wasn't sure just what she was thanking him for, and neither apparently was he, for his 'Thank you?' was so incredulous she laughed.

'It was a nice kiss,' she offered, hoping to keep things light between them.

'A nice kiss? Was that all you felt? No fire? No heat? No wanting?'

The fire, heat and wanting all escalated once again, but no way could she admit to them—

hating to admit them even to herself—because this neediness weakened her resolve and laughed at her attempted independence.

Why?

She wasn't sure. A relationship—a physical relationship—needn't weaken her.

Need it?

One kiss and she was thinking relationship?

With Flynn?

Was she mad?

Mind whirling with doubts and questions for which she had no answers, she pushed gently against the arms that still held her captive, backing out of that tempting embrace, away from the exciting warmth of his body.

He released her—far too easily—then put his hand around her shoulders and guided her back on to the driveway.

'My car's around the back. I'll take you back to the showground.'

She didn't protest, contrarily sorry now the kisses had ended but knowing they would probably resume in the privacy of his vehicle. Wanting them to resume…

Not wanting to want them…

Flashing lights interrupted her fantasy, turning

the moonlit night into a carnival. She heard Flynn sigh, felt his arm squeeze her shoulders, then he kissed her on the temple and turned away.

'I'll come with you. Maybe I can help,' she offered, hurrying beside him as he strode back into the hospital, turning left towards A and E, arriving there as the ambulance bearers opened the rear door of their vehicle.

'It's Mrs Warren. She was lifting a pot of boiling stock and it slopped over and spilled all down her leg,' Julie told Flynn, as he drew close enough to see the patient he'd released only two days earlier moaning in pain on the trolley.

Guilt that he'd given in to Mrs Warren's pleas to let her out of hospital a few days early hit him like a fist in the belly. Had it been festival fever that had caused him to make such a rash decision?

'Oh, Flynn, my hip,' Mrs Warren wailed, grabbing Flynn's hand and holding it tightly in both of hers. 'Tell me I haven't hurt my hip.'

One glance had shown him the extent of her burns, down both thighs and the lower right leg, yet she was worried about her hip?

'Did you fall, that you're worried about it?' he

asked her, still studying the burns, visible through the plastic wrap the ambos had applied.

'I kind of bumped myself,' she said, refusing to relinquish Flynn's hand, so he had to walk beside the trolley as it was wheeled in to A and E. 'I don't care about the burns but I need my hip to be all right. I couldn't go through all that again.'

'It's not likely you'll have hurt it—remember your new hip joint is far stronger than the old one was,' he reminded her, knowing she needed the reassurance, although the burns were in the fore-front of his mind.

Hot liquid—scalds—usually caused deep partial or full-thickness burns, depending on the temperature of the liquid and the length of time the skin was exposed to it. The fact that Mrs Warren was more concerned about her hip than the burns suggested they were at least deep-partial, generally less painful in the first instance than superficial burns.

Majella was standing at the entrance to the cubicle where he'd examined her earlier, the door open to allow them easy access.

'I'm good with burns,' she said, and though Flynn wondered about the ethics of allowing her to stay—after all, he only had her word that she had training of some kind—the way she spoke told him she could be useful.

'We started a drip, irrigated the wounds with saline, covered them with plastic film and brought her straight here,' Julie reported, handing the nurse who'd appeared Mrs Warren's papers, and getting a signature on the ambulance service's copy.

'Do you want me to call someone in?' the A and E nurse asked Flynn. 'I'm officially on duty in here tonight but you wanted me to stay near Sam and his family—especially with the new baby—so what do you think?'

'Majella's had experience with burns,' he said, only realising he'd made the decision to accept her help when he heard his own words. 'You can go back to Sam and the family—but stay unobtrusive.'

The nurse grinned at him.

'They're in the family room—of course I'll be unobtrusive.'

She disappeared and Flynn turned to his new assistant.

'Oxygen first?' she asked, lifting a mask and sliding it into place when he nodded.

'Then full obs—you do pulse and temp, I'll do the BP.'

'We'll sort out the burn, Mrs Warren,' he continued, 'then X-ray that hip to make sure it's still where it should be.'

Mrs Warren nodded, her eyelids drooping as if the ordeal had made her very tired.

'Stay with us, love,' Majella urged her. 'We need to ask you where it hurts, things like that, and after we're all done with questions, you can sleep.'

'Pulse is ninety-seven,' she said more quietly to Flynn.

'Could be mild hypoxia—her respiration rate is up as well. The oxygen should stabilise her fairly quickly.'

He was pumping up the blood-pressure cuff as he spoke, and the frown on his face as he watched the pressure register on the meter suggested it, too, was elevated.

'I'm going to run the fluid into you a little faster,' he told Mrs Warren. 'And as soon as we've examined your legs, I can give you a little more pain relief.'

He turned again to Majella.

'What's your estimation of the wound area?'

She smiled at him.

'Think I don't know the Rule of Nines, huh?'

she teased, the accompanying smile making him forget for an instant where they were.

'Leg's are nine per cent each, front and back and half the right leg is affected so I'd say five, and the left leg only partially burned, I'd say three—total eight, which isn't too bad.'

Flynn who was peeling off the plastic wrap nodded his agreement.

'Thickness?' he asked, and Majella came closer, peering over his shoulder at the burns.

'Skin pale and shiny,' she observed. 'Some blisters already developing, which means there's capillary destruction and fluid escaping to cause them. Could be some nerve damage as well, which is why they're not as painful as superficial burns.'

He nodded his agreement of her assessment, then spoke to Mrs Warren.

'I'm going to touch you in a couple of places and want you to tell me if the touch is blunt or sharp.'

He used his gloved finger to press down on some of the pale, avascular areas of the burn on the right leg, and was pleased when Mrs Warren's response was correct. He used the blunt end of a scalpel to press for sharp and again she could tell, but when he repeated the exercise on her left leg, which seemed less severely affected, she became confused, finally admitting she couldn't tell.

The skin above the burn on the left side was tight and shiny red, the redness suggesting superficiality. But now Flynn had to wonder.

'There are more blisters on her left leg,' Majella said, picking up on his uncertainty. 'Will you aspirate the fluid?'

'Have you done that in practice or just read about it?' he asked her, wondering just how far her training went.

'We try to do it always. I think I mentioned I spent time in Asia after that big earthquake there. We set up a field hospital and burn wounds were the most common thing we treated, not from fires after the earthquake but from cooking or heating fires. The theory we follow is that open wounds lose far more fluid than closed ones and are more susceptible to infection, so taking the roof off the blister is bad for two reasons. But then you get blisters which, by their very weight, create a bigger wound, so we go with getting rid of the fluid and leaving the skin intact.'

'Me, too,' Flynn said, although part of his mind

had picked up the least important bit of the conversation. Majella in Asia! In their youth, he'd been the one who'd wanted to travel—to see the world. All Majella had ever hankered for had been a home of her own.

Which was what she'd found in that small cave, a secret place—a home.

Yet she'd had a home…

Disquiet he couldn't pinpoint filtered through Flynn's mind and although he concentrated on Mrs Warren, part of his brain probed through memories of the past—little cameos of his youth, Majella's youth.

Work.

'You want to do that leg?' he asked his new assistant.

Majella looked at him in horror.

'Right now? Before you've given Mrs Warren some pain relief?'

'Almost right now,' he said. 'The opioid I slipped into the drip earlier should be working in a minute. Can you see the instruments you'll need?'

Was he testing her? Majella wondered, then she realised she couldn't blame him if he was. What did he know of her training or experience?

She found a tray and set out what she'd need on it, sterile pads, saline to rinse away the aspirate, and a syringe with a wide-bore needle. Saw Flynn nod and felt a sense of excitement as she realised they were working as a team.

'I'm going to take some of the fluid from the blisters on your legs,' she told Mrs Warren. 'I'll be as quick as I can, so Flynn can take you into X-Ray and check your hip.'

But working under Flynn's steady gaze made her fingers tremble and she was annoyed with herself for not doing the job as efficiently as she'd have liked, although Flynn's 'Well done' seemed genuine, his praise bringing delight in a way no official commendation had ever done.

With the blisters flattened into grey areas of damaged skin, and the wounds once again covered to prevent infection, they wheeled Mrs Warren through to X-Ray.

'Do you always do your own portering at night?' Majella asked him.

'Own portering, own X-rays, sometimes own nursing as well,' he said, sounding annoyed about the situation but accepting of it. 'Staff cuts are everywhere, and though we have plenty of beds and great equipment, we can't do a lot of more complicated medicine because we can't afford the staff. Mrs Warren had to go into Bendigo for her hip replacement, although she did come back here to recuperate. We've good physio services from two physios who job-share, each of them working five-day fortnights, and a visiting occupational therapist once a fortnight. She gives our staff exercises for patients to do and sees people here as outpatients.'

She helped him settle Mrs Warren into position beneath the machine, marvelling at his firm but gentle touch, his teasing care and evident concern. Once satisfied his patient was positioned properly but comfortable, he retreated behind the glassed screen, motioning for Majella to come with him.

He took two films then they shifted Mrs Warren to a different position so he could take another two. Flynn left to put them in the developer while Majella chatted to the now sleepy woman, trying to keep her mind off possible damage to her new hip joint.

'The hip's fine,' Flynn announced, coming back out with films which he put up in a light box so Mrs Warren would not only hear but see that all was well.

She'd probably seen so many X-rays of her hip she could read them herself, Majella realised.

'Now we'll settle you into bed,' Flynn told her, taking up the role of both porter and nurse once again, but when they reached a corridor that Majella hadn't been down before, a nurse came out to help them. Flynn and Majella helped her transfer Mrs Warren to a bed, then reattach her to her drip and oxygen.

'Did you drive up?' Flynn asked, guiding Majella out of the room while the nurse changed her patient into a nightgown.

It took Majella a moment to remember that she had. She smiled at him.

'I'd forgotten that,' she said. 'I'd have felt a right goose if I'd let you drive me back to the cabin then realised I'd left my own car at the hospital.'

'I don't think either of us were thinking straight at the time,' he said, and the look in his eyes as he spoke made her remember all the feelings the kiss had generated.

Could a look do that?

'I'd better go,' she said quickly, needing to get away from him so she could cool down and think rationally about all this. 'You're going home yourself?'

He shook his head.

'There are plenty of empty beds. I'll nap up here—I want to keep an eye on Mrs Warren. There's a danger with pain relief for burns victims so I can only give her small doses at regular intervals. Nitrous oxide is actually the best because it can be self-administered, but as she's a little hypoxic I can't give her that. Just small doses of opioid as she needs them.'

Majella lifted a hand and touched his shoulder.

'Try to get some sleep. It's been a long day.'

He smiled at her, the movement of his lips emphasising the lines age and tiredness had drawn in his face, although, if anything they made him more handsome.

'I will,' he promised, then he bent his head and kissed her on the lips. 'You too!'

Majella walked away, the tiredness she'd seen in Flynn's face now dogging her own footsteps. But she couldn't let a little tiredness fog her brain. She had to think, to consider where things now stood.

To consider the complication that was Flynn…

CHAPTER SIX

SMALL towns! Majella thought, as she, Helen and Sophie fought to keep the crowd around their stall happy. But although everyone who stopped there bought something—well, they really needed an excuse to stop and chat—she knew they were there for only one reason—to see the child they'd once seen in church all grown up.

'You rescued those little boys—that was brave,' one woman said, her restless hands pointing to first a soap and then a jar of salve. 'Of course, I knew your grandfather quite well. Yes, one of those green tubes, too. Will you be coming back to stay?'

'Are you OK?' Sophie whispered to her, as Majella turned to the back of the stall to bag the woman's purchases and sort out some change.

'I'm fine and we're making a fortune. At this

rate we'll sell out today and we can all go home tomorrow.'

She'd spoken unthinkingly, or perhaps thinking of her own escape, so Sophie's wail, 'And miss the ball?' brought her back down to earth.

'Of course not,' she promised, knowing Sophie had a new dress bought especially for this occasion—the farewell ball on the final evening of the festival—and quite possibly for the young man whose mother practised ayurvedic medicine in another of the stalls.

She turned back to the counter to give her customer her package and change, then moved on to the next one, another person more excited by the gossip that Majella Goldsworth had returned to Parragulla than the rescue of the boys or Helen's wonderful products.

Used to being just a number in the army, she found the attention trying, while the most frequently asked question—should she do up a list of FAQs and answers on a poster and hang it in front of the stall?—about whether she would return to live in Parragulla, was one she couldn't answer.

She'd been so excited when she'd seen the house advertised for auction. It had come at a time when she'd decided she had to make a home of her own. Somewhere! The ad had been like a sign—a confirmation that going back to Parragulla was the right move along the path to independence. She'd thought long and hard about it, wondering if she was making too much of a coincidence, but in the end the decision to return had felt right. The idea of turning the house into a happy, joy-filled home and cleansing it of the shadows of the past had begun to burn inside her.

But now she knew the house was beyond her reach, and what with Flynn and lost boys and kisses and Mrs Warren's burns, she hadn't had time to think about alternative futures.

'Man!' Gracie cried out, in such delighted tones Majella turned towards the playpen.

The little girl was standing up, pointing at an approaching figure.

A figure so familiar the embers of attraction lit last night flared back to life in Majella's body.

'Flynn!' she murmured, but he hadn't noticed her, all his attention on the small girl who called to him.

'Man!' Grace was shouting now and holding up her hands towards Flynn.

'Little flirt!' Helen said fondly, but the child's behaviour was disturbing to Majella, and not only because of Grace's lack of discrimination in choosing which man to smile at.

Majella had always known her daughter would need some stable male influences in her life as she was growing up, but hadn't thought a three-year-old would differentiate between the sexes, simply being happy to have people who loved her inhabiting her small world.

To Majella's surprise, Flynn had responded to the upraised arms, and her daughter now rested on his arm, while her soft baby lips whispered secrets in his ear and her chubby baby hands clutched his head.

Pain she didn't understand shafted through Majella's body and she closed her eyes, but the image of the man and child seemed burnt onto her retinas and refused to go away.

'Not that pink soap, the yellow one,' a customer said, and Majella turned her mind back to selling soap, although with Grace in Flynn's arms some of her attention was on him.

She concluded the sale of yellow soap, smiling politely but not terribly sincerely.

'Six cakes of lemon myrtle soap, please.'

Now *all* of her attention was on him, and on Grace who was pointing to the man she'd snavelled as if introducing him to her mother!

'Shades of things to come,' Helen whispered in Majella's ear, and Majella spun towards her friend.

'What do you mean?' she demanded, so abruptly Helen took a step back.

'Teenage years,' Helen said mildly. 'Bringing the boyfriend home to meet Mum!'

'Oh!'

Feeling stupid, Majella packed the six cakes of soap into a paper bag, then handed them to Flynn, holding out her arms for her daughter at the same time.

'Don't you trust me with her?' he asked, jiggling Grace up and down on his arm so the child squealed with delight.

'I wouldn't trust you with any woman still breathing,' Helen answered for Majella. 'Not with that smile.'

The teasing statement made Majella look at him again, seeing what Helen saw—a tall, rangy, very good-looking guy with sleepy blues eyes and a sinfully sexy smile.

What on earth had she been thinking, kissing him last night?

Apart from the emotional tumult it had caused her, men who looked like Flynn would always have a woman in their lives.

And he still held her child.

'I'm going to talk to someone about windmills and wind power. Maybe Grace would like a change of scenery.'

It was a challenge—will you trust your child to me?—and Majella knew it. What she couldn't understand was why he'd want to lug a child along with him when he was off to do man things with windmills.

'They have miniatures set up in front of a fan, demonstrating the way they work and how much power they generate. Grace might like them.'

Grace would love them, but that didn't lessen the uneasiness that sat heavily in Majella's chest.

'So is this Flynn?' Sophie joined them, breaking a silence that was becoming very strained.

At least embarrassment was better than confusion, and with heated cheeks Majella introduced her friends.

'I met Flynn yesterday,' Helen announced. 'We introduced ourselves. But I'd like to see the windmills working. OK if I come along as well?'

Grace apparently approved this idea, beaming at Helen and patting her head, saying, 'Nana!' in a pleased voice but remaining contentedly perched on Flynn's arm.

Now Helen was included in the expedition, Majella could hardly object, but as she watched them walk away, Grace's head resting trustfully on Flynn's shoulder, uneasiness was so strong it was close to nausea roiled in her stomach and her hands shook as she handed creams and salves and soap to customers, and smiled, and took their money.

'RSI,' she said to Sophie a little later. 'First recorded case of repetitive strain injury in the cheek muscles from smiling all the time.'

'It does feel like that, but the stall's doing really well,' Sophie said, checking there were no customers in sight for once and giving Majella a quick hug. 'So, what about the house?'

Majella smiled, a real smile this time, not the one that put her in danger of getting RSI.

'Your mother's been so tactful—she hasn't said a word—but typical teenager, you had to ask!'

'Well, someone had to,' Sophie protested. 'You're not exactly the most forthcoming of people, now, are you? Not into sharing your thoughts or feelings! If a person didn't ask you stuff, she'd never learn anything. So what are you thinking?'

Majella considered the question for a moment, then answered honestly.

'The honest truth is I can't afford it. Whether there's another house here I can afford, or whether I really want to settle here if I can't have that house, I don't know. I don't seem to be able to think clearly about any of it.'

'You can't afford a house that should have been yours anyway?' Sophie's voice betrayed her opinion of such injustice. 'That's ridiculous. So what next?'

'I can't decide—can't seem to make a decision at all,' Majella admitted, and Sophie gave her a quick hug.

'Mental block?'

'Something like that,' Majella told her, although she knew it wasn't anything to do with the house that she couldn't think about it, but to do with Flynn and the way thoughts of him were consuming all her brain cells, and causing hot and bothersome problems in her other cells as well.

Maybe thinking about the house was a good idea—thinking about *a* house, any house—and the independence she was seeking. She searched inside herself for the impetus that had driven this return to Parragulla but it had apparently been consumed by the heat she'd been experiencing.

'Stupid, stupid, stupid,' she muttered to herself, realising how easily she'd become distracted from her plan—how easily she'd drifted off course.

Flynn only half listened to Helen's chat as they made their way towards the marquee housing the technical exhibits. Only this time his distraction wasn't caused by memories of the kiss he'd shared with Majella the previous evening but by the soft, cuddly bundle of charm on his arm—by the trusting arms clasping him, and the sweet baby scent of the feathery curls that tickled his chin.

Why had he picked the child up?

And having done so, why was he walking through the showground with her?

He'd been trying to find Majella since the old man had died—or since he'd learned the contents of the old man's will—but having found her, why had things become so difficult? This question of marriage. A brief phone call to the solicitor had failed to approve Flynn's contention that having been married would qualify Majella to inherit the house.

He tried to think logically about the situation. Her husband had been dead three years. She could well have a new man in her life. There was a month before the old man's deadline. She could get married again.

But as she'd already objected to the manipulation inherent in the condition, would she marry to satisfy it? He doubted it. Although she didn't know the rest of it—about the money that came with the house, or the money in trust for this happy child he held in his arms and in trust for future children Majella might have.

Would she be stubborn enough to deny her children money that would secure their futures?

The thought of her having more babies caused nearly as much inner discomfort as the thought of her having a man in her life had only minutes earlier.

But forgetting that and getting back to the will, the fact remained he had to talk to her.

They'd both been busy, he excused himself as guilt that he hadn't mentioned more about the will swamped through him. Worst time of the year, festival time, but as Majella's child nuzzled his neck and whispered, 'Man!' into his ear, he knew there was more to it than being busy.

Seeing Majella again had spun him into some limbo between the past and present, while kissing Majella had—well, the only way he could think to phrase it was that it had blown his mind.

Done equally traumatic stuff to the rest of his body as well...

'You're not listening to a word I'm saying, are you?' Helen demanded, as they drew close to the windmill stall and Grace began to crow with delight at the moving model.

'Not really,' he admitted, and she gave him the kind of look he usually got from Belle, or his mother, or one of his sisters.

'I was asking about the house. Majella says it's far too expensive for her to buy. I have a little money put by—maybe I could help. But it would have to be between the two of us—if she knew I was offering it, she'd get back on this independent thing and refuse.'

Now Helen had his full attention, or almost full attention. The little bundle of delight in his arms had captured part of it.

He knew he shouldn't have picked her up!

'It's actually been left to her but with conditions,' he said to Helen, concentrating on his reply because there was a lot of confusion in his head. 'It should be hers anyway. The problem is there's a time limit for passing it over, and if that's not met, it's to be auctioned. We've been searching for her for eleven months without success. With the time limit approaching, we had to advertise the auction. I did wonder if perhaps the auction ads might bring her back, even though other pleas for information had failed.'

'Well, we were coming for the festival, but the ads did attract her attention,' Helen asked. 'And now she's here?'

He looked blankly at her and received another incredulous look.

'You must have had some reason for wanting her back in town,' Helen prompted.

'So I could explain about the will,' Flynn said.

'Oh, yes?' Disbelieving look this time, making Flynn realise he'd never actually analysed his reasons for his mad search for Majella. Up front, yes, he was executor of the will, so it was his duty, but the search had become an obsession with him and he didn't think he could blame his executorial duties for that.

Best he ignore Helen's taunt.

'Look, Gracie! See how the little arms go round.'

He knelt and set the little girl on the ground, keeping his hands protectively close to her, ready to stop any sudden move towards the slowly turning models, concentrating on the child, not the churning thoughts Helen's probing had stirred up in his head.

'And *have* you talked to her about it? Properly? Sat down and discussed it with her?'

Typical woman, Helen had no intention of letting the subject drop, although she'd been diverted for a short time by the salesman giving her literature on the efficacy of wind power.

'I told her about the conditions,' Flynn said, lifting Grace who'd lost interest in the windmills and looked ready to take off through the forest of legs in front of the display. 'Well, some of them.'

'Conditions?'

Helen sounded startled enough for Flynn to realise Majella hadn't mentioned the conditions to her friend.

'It's complicated,' Flynn said. 'But there's been so much going on we haven't had a proper talk.'

'Why not take her out to dinner and discuss it, then?' Helen suggested, and, as Grace distracted him with wet kisses on his cheek, he found himself saying yes, he thought he would, though the surge of joy he felt was immediately squelched when Helen added, 'Not that she'll take kindly to conditions set by that man, her grandfather. For Majella, this whole return to Parragulla deal is about independence, and if he's tied her to him somehow, she'd hate that. Sophie and I would love to have her and Grace stay with us for ever, but Majella feels she's leant on us for far too long. And though that's not true, I do understand her need to prove something to herself.'

'Surely she's proved herself often enough during her army career?' Flynn protested.

'Proved herself an efficient officer and an efficient medic, yes, but as a person? She always said her childhood was perfect training for the army, with her autocratic grandfather, the rules and regulations of boarding school, and bossy Flynn giving her orders all the time.'

'Bossy Flynn?' Flynn questioned, but Helen only smiled at him.

They'd arrived back at the stall, where Majella was explaining to a group of schoolchildren about the network of volunteers that kept the Native Animal Rescue Service going.

'Flynn wants you to have dinner with him tonight,' Helen announced, forestalling any idea on Flynn's part to back out of the date. 'Sophie and I will be happy to mind Grace.'

'You've been minding Grace ever since we arrived,' Majella protested as the schoolchildren departed, clutching bumper stickers and information leaflets.

'That's one of the reasons we came,' Helen reminded her, and for the first time since the conversation had begun, Majella looked directly at Flynn.

'Do you always get someone else to do your asking?' she murmured, her tone teasing, although he could see tension in the way she stood and hear it in the sharpness of her own voice.

Flynn put Grace down on the ground and watched her run, arms outstretched, towards her mother.

'I'd like to talk to you about a number of things—business things,' he said to her, then held out his hands in supplication. 'Would you please have dinner with me tonight?'

Would she? Majella wondered. Should she?

Dinner meant night-time and right now the full moon came along with darkness. It wasn't moon madness Majella feared but the enhancing effect of moonlight on romance—although Flynn's invitation had definitely been practical, not romantic.

And practically speaking, she needed to sort out some things with Flynn—he'd mentioned other conditions in the will…

'OK, what time and where? I'll meet you. That way, if you get called out I can get myself home.'

He seemed startled, as if the last thing he'd expected had been her acquiescence. She smiled, pleased she'd startled him.

'Eight would be good. There's a top restaurant, Rosem—'

He stopped halfway through the word, frowned at her, then shrugged.

'Come to dinner at my place. You're right about the possibility of being called out. But if we're at my place you can stay and finish your meal in your own time, and it won't be as bad as being left like a shag on a rock in the middle of the restaurant.'

Shag on a rock in the middle of a restaurant? Mixed metaphors?

But she kind of knew what he meant.

'Where's your place? As executor, are you living at Parragulla House? It looked well cared for.'

He was frowning at her as if she should know, and she tried to remember if she had noticed any signs of habitation. As far as she could recall, it had felt empty and abandoned, but she'd been thrown by Flynn's presence, so…

'No, but a housekeeper goes in every week. I bought a place up near the hospital. From the showground, you go out to the main road then first turn to the left. Mine's the place at the end of the road.'

Which didn't really explain the frown, but Majella nodded, then, feeling Grace growing heavy in her arms, she assured him she'd find it and excused herself to put the little one down for a sleep.

Flynn walked away, curiously dissatisfied with the arrangement, wishing he could take Majella somewhere special, somewhere like Rosemary's, which was the best restaurant in town, but given he'd taken Rosemary out a few times since she'd shifted to Parragulla, and he knew, as far as she was concerned, they were dating, he could hardly take another woman there.

Rosemary!

There had been too many Rosemary's in his life. Attractive, intelligent, vibrant women with whom he'd enjoyed pleasant, at times even exciting relationships. But though he would no longer put his reluctance to marry in the words Majella had recited to him, the doubts and cynicism about wedded bliss, or even wedded harmony, must still be there, ingrained deep within him, because all of the relationships had fizzled out, lacking sufficient impetus to take the next step towards commitment.

Lacking sufficient passion?

Where had that word come from?

It was lust raked heat through a man's body from time to time—not passion...

He wandered aimlessly through the marquee. He was dithering—he who never dithered...

He turned around and walked back towards the Nature's Wonders stall. He'd talk to Majella now about the will, take her and Grace for a walk out behind the marquees, somewhere quiet, and explain it all. That way tonight could be...

A date?

Customers still crowded around the stall, and Flynn guessed a lot of the questions they were asking were about Majella and personal. She seemed pale and he waited until she'd finished serving an older woman, then beckoned to her.

'Hey, Doc! Fancy seeing you here!' Paul Blair, a recent recruit to the ambulance service—a local who even as a child had been a cocky little bugger—greeted Flynn then turned towards Majella who was approaching the pair of them on the other side of the counter. 'And who's your pretty friend? Don't tell me this is the long-lost heiress? Wow! She's not a dog at all! Are you going to marry her? Does Rosemary know?'

Flynn stared at the young man in disbelief, then realised he was probably paraphrasing whatever gossip was all over town. He knew no one in the solicitor's office would have talked of the conditions of the will, but information seemed to leak out by osmosis.

By the time he'd found some stern words about gossiping to say to the young man, Paul had disappeared into the crowd.

'Why would he ask if you were going to marry me?' Majella demanded in a husky whisper, leaning over the counter towards Flynn while her eyes followed Paul as he moved away. 'Does the whole town know about that stupid will?'

'They shouldn't. That kind of thing is confidential, but somehow bits and pieces leak out, usually all wrong,' Flynn said helplessly. 'Small country town talk—it's like Chinese whispers!'

But he could see from her frown she wasn't satisfied. Which was all the more reason to talk to her now.

But this idea was foiled by the musical notes of his mobile, and he lifted it to his ear to hear a summons to the hospital.

'I've got to go,' he said to Majella. 'I'll see you later. Eightish?'

Majella watched him go, her mind on the conversation.

Why had that lad asked Flynn if they'd be marrying? Presumably people had heard about the 'happy marriage' clause in the old man's will. Were they assuming that Flynn, as executor, would have the best chance of marrying her for the house? Or was there some other condition she didn't know about? She wouldn't have put it past her grandfather to have specified a particular husband—or type of husband—but doubted he'd have wanted his disappointing granddaughter to marry Flynn, a boy the old man had always held in high esteem.

Or was it just that Flynn was still single? That with her return, the town was imagining he'd been carrying the pain of lost love in his heart?

As if!

Although now the words 'lost love' were bouncing up and down in her head. Could that be what was wrong with her—what had made her love for Jeff caring, warm, and companionable but not abuzz with passion?

Puzzling over passion—did it even exist?—she made her way back to the stall.

Shivering when she remembered last night's kiss.

Did passion make you shiver?

Flynn drove up to the hospital, his mind darting from one thought to another, concentration difficult, although it didn't take much brain power to read the most recent obs on Mrs Warren. An infection, almost inevitable in burns, had set in, and he had to change the antibiotics she was getting in her drip, strengthening the dose and adding a second infection fighter to the mix.

He checked the wounds, wondering if he'd

need to take the skin off one of them, then deciding he'd leave it to see if the change in the drug regime worked.

As he was at the hospital, he'd walk through and check how everyone was.

Hopefully, the few patients who were in residence would all be well, and no emergency calls would disturb his evening with Majella.

CHAPTER SEVEN

NERVOUS as a teenager on a first date, Flynn looked around his living room. A small fire—it wasn't really cool enough for a fire but it looked homely—burned in the stone hearth, and the lamps he'd lit shone pools of light, softening the bareness of the room—a cast-off lounge suite, a big recliner and a small coffee-table the sum total of its furniture.

But the casserole simmering in the oven smelled good, and the dining table, an antique he'd bought because he'd loved it from the moment he'd set eyes on it in a shop window, set with silver and crystal, looked great.

He was ready.

And his hands were shaking…

He had to get past this physical reaction to Majella—had to think of her as a friend or, better still, as an acquaintance with whom he had some business to transact. But his next glance around the living room took in the little chest—sitting in the middle of the mantelpiece above the fire, the letter tucked beneath it.

As well as explaining the terms of the will, he had to give her the letter and the chest.

Paralysed down his right side by a stroke, two weeks after Majella had disappeared, the old man had never recovered the use of his right hand. Further strokes had left him bedridden for the last years of his life and, knowing the end was near, he'd summoned Flynn one day—not Flynn the doctor, but Flynn the boy who'd worked for him.

Flynn had watched as he'd painstakingly written Majella's name on the envelope with his left hand then he'd handed Flynn the envelope and a little chest, indicating through grunts and gestures that he wanted Flynn to find his granddaughter and pass both on to her.

Flynn had brought them home and put them on the mantelpiece, where they'd waited, like a time-bomb...

The old man's death had been well publicised—former race horse owner, famed breeder of working dogs, wealthy property owner—and both the solicitors and Flynn had waited for Majella to come forward, but no one had heard a word, the funeral had gone ahead, the will read and the solicitors' duties had ended. It had been up to Flynn, as executor, to find her.

And he'd tried, had hired a private investigator, but had failed to discover a trace of her, although now Flynn knew she'd been in the army, that was more understandable. Where could one be swallowed up more easily than in the armed forces?

Flynn slid the letter out from beneath the little chest and tapped it against the palm of his hand. Knowing now how the old man had treated Majella, he wondered if the letter would contain more pain.

Could he not give it to her?

The sound of an approaching vehicle made him tuck the letter back beneath the chest before walking out to his front veranda to welcome her inside.

She took the two steps to his veranda in one long stride, then turned to look around her.

'Well, it's close to the hospital, I suppose,' Majella said, and he could read her doubt about the little place he'd bought.

'It is that,' he agreed. 'And it's all mine. You

have no idea how good it was to have a bathroom to myself after growing up with two sisters.'

Majella studied him, trying to figure out his mood, or maybe the tone he was setting for the evening.

A meeting of old friends?

A business discussion?

Not a date, that was for sure—his demeanour was far too casual.

Although, hopefully, she appeared equally at ease, for all that her insides were twisted tighter than a seaman's knot.

'Come on in.'

The front door lacked a porch or entry so you stepped straight into the living room. The fire was nice, but the room was so bare of personality Majella turned to study Flynn again. The young Flynn had left his mark wherever he'd gone—to have not marked his house as a home seemed peculiar.

'So, welcome to my home,' he said, and now the scent of something cooking—something delicious—made it seem more homely.

Flynn tried to see the place through her eyes, and was disappointed, although when she saw the dining-room table...

'In the army you don't really have a home,' she said quietly, and Flynn felt a bruising in his heart at the sadness of the thought.

But tonight was for practical matters, not bruised hearts.

'Well, you can have one now—Parragulla House is yours, Majella. We'll sort out the details somehow. Come into the dining room, we'll discuss it over dinner.'

He stepped through the divider between the two rooms and bent to light the candles on the dining table.

Then turned.

She came towards him, so lithe and lovely it was all he could do not to take her in his arms.

The house! Sort out the house first, his head reminded him, so, instead of kissing her, he took her elbow and guided her inside.

'How lovely!'

No way could Majella stop her exclamation of delight, but the beautifully set table—and the candles—conjured up romance, not practicality, and the confused emotions jostling within her made her feel shaky and uncertain.

Though at least with this furniture and setting, she'd found where Flynn *had* made his mark.

He'd excused himself, returning with two bottles of wine, offering her a choice of white or red.

'I'm no connoisseur so you choose,' she told him, telling herself she'd do no more than sip politely at whatever he poured, because alcohol would only confuse her more.

He opened the bottle of red and set it on the table, then pulled out a chair and held it for her.

So formal, so composed, she began to wonder if she'd imagined the kiss they'd shared the previous evening, or if she'd read too much into it.

But then her body brushed against his as she took her seat, and she heard his sharp intake of air, and a half-swallowed curse.

'Flynn?'

She sat, but turned to look up at him, and saw desire leaping in his eyes, partnered by restraint in the clenched muscles in his jaw.

'Business—it's business tonight, Majella,' he muttered at her. He went out to the kitchen and returned a few minutes later, setting down a plate in front of her—a good hearty country meal, some kind of casserole chock full of vegetables, served with mashed potatoes, peas and carrots.

'Meat and three veg! You've done well,' she

said, deciding she had to pretend to be as unaffected by the kiss as he was. 'Do you enjoy cooking?'

He smiled. 'Not to the extent of watching cooking shows on TV, but during seven years at university, I'd have died of starvation if I hadn't learned some basic skills. And with doctoring, I've found anything I can cook in the oven is best, as it can stay there through long delays and only gets better with extra cooking.'

'Life in the army meant I didn't have to learn to cook,' she told him, 'so my culinary skills began with strained vegetables, which I learned for Grace, and now I've progressed to grilling a small lamb chop or poaching a chicken breast.'

She tucked into the meal, pronounced it delicious, then surreptitiously watched Flynn eat. She knew she shouldn't be feeling delight in such innocent voyeurism, yet she was fascinated by the economic movement of his hands and by the way his lips moved and how a muscle bunched in his jaw as he chewed.

'I don't suppose I ever saw you eat.'

The words were out before she could stop them, and he looked up, startled, as well he might be.

She waved her hand, as if to wipe out the

foolish sentence, but his blue eyes still questioned the remark.

'It *was* a strange friendship—ours,' she added, hoping he'd understand the path her mind had taken.

Pleased when he smiled.

'It was,' he agreed, 'which is where we can begin.'

He set down his knife and fork and pushed his plate, not quite cleaned up, away from him.

'When the old man died, I hired a private investigator to find you, but he had no luck, then when it was time to advertise the house for the auction I wondered if perhaps you might come back, if only for a look.'

Flynn watched her closely as he spoke, but her face, though pale, revealed nothing of what she might be thinking.

'I changed my name—that's why your man didn't find me,' she said quietly. 'Thinking Grandfather might send someone to look for me, I changed it straight away—that first night.'

She offered a half-smile so pathetic Flynn felt the bruising in his heart again.

'Tell me where you went,' he prompted, needing to know—needing reassurance she'd been all right, although it was now so long ago. 'What happened? All of it, not bits and pieces.'

A better smile this time.

'Maybe not all,' she said, then took a deep breath and began.

'When I left Parragulla, I hitched for a while, then the car I was in—I only got in with families—hit a koala and the father, who was driving, said it would be dead, but I'd seen the signs for the rescue service as Bill drove me back and forth to school and for some reason I'd memorised the number. I thought we should ring someone, so I told them I was only going to the next village and got out, found a public phone and rang the number. Didn't I already tell you this? Anyway, Helen answered. I explained I had no transport but was going to walk back to where we'd hit the animal and she came to collect it, and collected me as well, and that's what happened.'

'Did the koala survive?' Flynn asked, while inside he was thanking whatever guardian angel Majella had for taking care of her that night— and thereafter?—in the best possible way.

Majella shook her head. 'I've found out since that koala's are hard to save,' she said. 'They've got such bulky bodies they can't move fast enough to get out of the way of cars, and the slightest of bumps seems to knock them out for hours. It's a bit like humans with brain injuries being in a coma—you don't know until they come out of it whether they'll have brain damage or not.'

'And if they do—the koalas?' Flynn asked, as his fascination with this new subject diverted him from the main issue of the tale.

'We have to put them down. A koala with brain damage that causes lack of co-ordination can't climb a tree, or if he does he'll probably fall out again.'

Flynn shook his head. Majella spoke so matter-of-factly, as if this was a perfectly normal conversation, yet to him it seemed bizarre to be discussing koalas with brain damage falling out of trees.

Especially in the context of the evening.

'You said you changed your name. Did you do it then? Give Helen a false name?'

To his surprise, Majella bent her head and suddenly became very interested in chasing a few remaining peas around her plate. A nod was all he got by way of answer, but after a few seconds she raised her head and said, 'I changed it legally, by deed poll later, so it didn't seem so much of a lie.'

'But you kept Majella? Helen calls you that.' She looked up at him, eyes defiant.

'That name was my mother's choice. It's just about the only thing Grandfather ever told me about her—that she'd given me what he called a stupid name. Of course I kept it.'

Flynn nodded his understanding, although his heart was hurting once again. Then, to divert his thoughts from pain, he went back a step.

'Changed your name to what?'

'Just changed it.' She shrugged and, as she searched for something else to attend to now all the peas were gone, he was certain she was hiding something.

'What did you change it to?' he persisted, puzzled that a name change should be disturbing her.

'Sinclair!' she muttered, then she looked up and glared at him. 'It was the first name that popped into my head.'

The words were so defensive Flynn had to laugh, but inside a rush of warmth suggested he found some special meaning in her choice.

'So now you know it all,' she said, as though this explanation of the night she'd fled encompassed the whole gamut of the missing years.

Not that he wanted to know about her marriage…

'Right up to now,' she added, 'when I came to Parragulla to buy the house.'

'Why?'

She frowned at him, dark brows drawing together over eyes that seemed pale as water in the candlelight.

'Why buy the house?'

He nodded. 'It seems strange that you'd want to buy it when you'd been so unhappy there.'

'But I told you,' Majella protested. 'It wasn't the house's fault I was unhappy. And there was something else—something you'll probably think is stupid—something I haven't even admitted fully to myself, let alone to Helen or anyone else. But since I had Grace—since I became a mother—I can't stop thinking about my own mother. I know so little about her, Flynn.'

Flynn heard her words and felt the sadness of them deep within his gut.

'Did my grandfather ever talk to you about my mother? Do you know anything about her? Did your mother ever tell you anything? Would she have known my mother?'

Flynn searched his mind. For sure, the old man

had never spoken of his daughter, but had his mother ever talked of her?

He shook his head, unable to find a single memory.

'I doubt anyone in town knew any more of her than they did of you,' he said, coming to squat beside Majella's chair so he could touch her knee and be close should she need his support. 'As far as I know, like you, she went to boarding school, coming home only in the long holidays. Old Bill always said she rode well so I guess the old man encouraged her to ride the way he did with you, but I imagine the only time anyone in town saw her was at church.'

'Then I was wrong,' Majella whispered. 'I always thought she must have been so happy, growing up at Parragulla House with a mother and a father—a real family—and I imagined that when her mother died Grandfather was so unhappy he made her unhappy as well and that's why she ran away.'

'But her mother died in childbirth. You must have known that, surely,' Flynn said, some memories returning, though how he knew this he couldn't have said.

The sudden paling of Majella's cheeks told

him she hadn't known and he stared at her, seeing the freckles darken on her skin, seeing the fragile beauty of this woman as she fought to keep her composure in this traumatic situation.

She won whatever inner battle she was fighting, and shrugged her shoulders, offering him a wry smile.

'So much for dreams, huh?' she said, then turned practical.

'Old Bill—is he still alive?'

Flynn shook his head.

'He died before your grandfather.'

'So there's no one who knew her I can ask.' She sighed. 'I kind of suspected that, but I couldn't help feeling if I was living in the house I'd be close to her.'

She tried a smile that failed completely, but as Flynn watched she straightened her shoulders, and took a deep breath.

'And the dog runs would have been ideal for the animals,' she said, as if the deviation into sentimentality had never happened.

She met his gaze.

'I'm committed to the rescue service, Flynn,' she said, and he could hear the sincerity in the words. 'Not only because it virtually rescued me, but because I'm good with animals. I discovered that when I was living with Helen—I've got an affinity with them. I'd have studied vet science if I'd been able to afford it, but even when I went into the army I always knew eventually I'd do something with animals.'

'And you can't live with Helen and do that? Isn't it what she does?'

'Now she's started the other business, she's cutting back on volunteer work. And with the business growing, she needs more room—a proper lab which could be set up in the room we use for operating. But that's not the point, I need something of my own—I need to prove to myself that I can stand alone and make a life for me and Grace.'

How could she go it alone—fend for herself and her child—when her life had been so proscribed, first by her grandfather, then by the Sherwoods, and finally within the army? Flynn thought, as protective feelings he was sure he'd lost when his two sisters had left home rose up within him once again.

'OK,' he said, although he couldn't really understand her determination. 'But you don't have to buy the house. It should be yours, Majella. It and all the money.'

'Money?'

She echoed the word so faintly he stared at her in disbelief.

'You must have known your grandfather had money—a lot of money.'

Majella frowned as she considered Flynn's words.

'I didn't ever think about it,' she said, shaking her head in wonder that she hadn't ever considered her grandfather's financial situation. 'I know boarding schools cost money, and he always insisted the housekeepers bought me good-quality clothes, but...'

She shrugged, unable to explain why she'd never given it a thought.

'Well, he did have money,' Flynn said.

'And?'

'It's also yours—well, some of it is.'

'Or it would have been if I was married,' Majella said tiredly. 'If poor Jeff hadn't been so foolish as to get himself killed in a flaming helicopter crash.'

'Oh, Majella!'

Flynn stood up and put his arm around her,

holding her as he had sometimes in the past—
Flynn the supportive friend.

He felt her tremble beneath his encircling arm,
and wondered if she was weeping as she pressed
her head into his shoulder.

Helicopter crash? Three years ago? And
suddenly he remembered the news reports—
Australian medical personnel on their way to
help, the helicopter crashing, killing all but one
or two on board…

Killing Majella's husband…?

'I know words are inadequate, but I'm so
sorry,' he whispered, brushing his hand across
her hair, teasing his fingers into its thickness,
feeling the silky strands against his skin.

She leant against him and he felt the tension
seeping out of her body, then she straightened,
touched his face and smiled.

'I am over it, you know, although you never
forget. There are things you can't forget. I would
have been with him, you see, if I hadn't been on
maternity leave. Grace was born the same day.
I lost Jeff and gained a daughter all at once, and
having Grace, having a helpless infant to take
care of, got me through for months, then I went
back to work, like getting back on a horse after

a fall, I suppose. But after the trip to Asia I realised I didn't want Grace growing up as an army brat, with me away for months on end, and the two of us always on the move. What I wanted for Grace was a home...'

A real home...

CHAPTER EIGHT

HE WRAPPED his arms around her, gently this time, responding to the sympathy he felt for her, not the attraction. She nestled against him, moving so both of them were standing, arms around each other, giving and receiving comfort, although she wasn't to know how much her story had hurt him—how much he needed the comfort.

The heat came later, surprising Flynn with it's sudden reappearance, and though the kisses he pressed on her lips were still gentle, it was getting harder to hide the reaction of his body.

Had Majella's blood also heated, that she pressed more closely? That her lips moved from accepting to demanding?

'Oh, Flynn,' she murmured, as his hands slid beneath her sweater, his fingers sliding up the knobs of her spine, snapping free her bra so he could hold and cup her heavy breasts.

He felt her hands seek beneath his shirt, urgent hands, reefing it from his trousers as if she needed to touch his skin right now.

Cool hands against his skin, soft hands, pressing his shoulder blades to bring him closer, her body arching into his, little breaths of sound coming from her lips as he teased one already peaking nipple.

Her hands were on his belt now, trying to unsnap his jeans.

'Bedroom,' he whispered in her ear, then he swung her into his arms and carried her in, hitting the light switch with his elbow as they entered the room.

'No lights,' she said, reaching out behind him to turn it off, then little else was said, both stripping silently, finding the bed, wrapped in each other's arms, Flynn's lips fully occupied exploring Majella's body, Majella's stopped by emotion so strong she could only gasp, or shiver, or sometimes give a little cry.

Beyond thought, Flynn explored her body—with lips and hands, learning what she liked and didn't like through little gasps and cries. His own body he held in check, but only just, and only until Majella reached for him, running her hands down his naked back, her hands cupping his buttocks, drawing him closer, one hand sliding around to hold and fondle him, guiding him into her body, primed by touch and feel for his invasion.

'Oh, Flynn,' he heard her whisper as he entered her with one swift, sure movement, then her legs clasped around his back and she joined him in the rhythmic dance of desire, setting the pace with her own movements, slowing him, then moving faster, until he couldn't bear it any longer.

He felt her release, her body shiver and give way beneath him, and the little cry she gave broke his restraint, though his cry was more a shout—curtailed swiftly to a groan.

He slumped across her body, sliding sideways so he wasn't smothering her, but keeping his arms around her—protective now—while his mind whirled with recriminations.

What the hell had he been thinking? He, who was so careful, had just had unprotected sex. And with Majella, of all people, who was as confused and unsure about their relationship and the future as he was.

* * *

She'd lost him, Majella realised as his body slid off hers. And though his arms still held her, as hers held him, she knew his thoughts were far from love, or lust, or sex, or whatever it was they'd just shared.

So, while her body sparked with remembered pleasure, and the warmth of Flynn's attentions still burned within her, her heart felt sad and heavy. It wasn't that she wanted promises of undying love—or even false assurances that love might have been involved in what had just occurred—but a touch, a caress, a whispered endearment wouldn't have gone astray.

The things she'd have liked to whisper dried to nothing on her tongue, and she eased away, eager to retrieve her clothes, to dress and get away so she could try to sort out what had happened far from Flynn's distracting presence.

The light came on—a bedside light—as she bent to feel among the scattered garments, and she heard the sharp intake of Flynn's breath then felt his fingers on her back.

On her scars…

'Your husband beat you?' The words were spoken quietly enough, but held such a mix of disbelief and anger that she turned to Flynn.

'Not my husband,' she whispered, and hoped her eyes didn't show remembered fear.

'Your grandfather?'

Flynn heard his incredulity in the two words, and knew this disbelief would hurt her, but how could he get his head around the idea of the man who'd been so good to him doing this to his own flesh and blood?

Majella had turned towards him so he could no longer see her back, but the image of the fine white lines criss-crossed the curves of her bottom, a few straying higher, one near her bra—fine as snail trails in the grass, old scars, but unmistakable as scars—stayed with Flynn.

He couldn't speak, his chest too full of pain and confusion. He simply stared at her, his mind a fog of conjecture mixed with random memories.

That pup is not a pet!

The cave.

Her treasures.

But the cave had become too small and eventually she'd fled.

He put one hand on her shoulder, the other on her chin, forcing her head up, looking at eyes hidden from him by her eyelids, dark feathery lashes fluttering on her pale cheeks. He touched the scar that ran across her temple.

'This, too?' he whispered, still not wanting to believe it possible—not wanting it to be the man who'd given Flynn so many opportunities.

She nodded.

'But why? What would you ever have done wrong?'

She raised her eyes to meet his and smiled at him, the kind of smile that would have broken a statue's heart.

'Running in the house, missing a chord in piano practice, a stain on a dress, a scuff on a new shoe—what didn't I do wrong?'

God damn him! Flynn roared, catching the words behind his lips and smothering them before they escaped and frightened her with their ferocity. 'Why did you not say? Not tell someone?'

'Tell who, Flynn?' she whispered. 'You, who thought him God? The housekeepers, who must have heard him whipping me, must have seen the strip of bamboo or riding crop he used. I think it's why so many left. And why he always employed them through a Melbourne agency, not locally. Who knows? Maybe every single one of them remonstrated with him.'

He had no answer except to take her in his arms and hold her close, hugging her and rocking her in his arms, wanting to take away pain she no longer felt, except in her heart—and in all the memories of her childhood.

'Oh, Majella,' he whispered into her unruly hair, 'why didn't you say? Why didn't you tell me?'

'What could you have done, Flynn? You worked for him to help your family—could you have got another job that paid as well? That paid at all, given your age when you first started working for him in the stables?'

She pushed away and pale green eyes scanned his face—pale green eyes full of sadness.

For the past? For what might have been?

'But you helped me, always, Flynn, just by being my friend,' she whispered, and the anger he'd stifled earlier burst forth.

'Your friend? Fine friend I turned out to be. Letting that man get away with such behaviour. And you!'

He glared at her, and although aware that she'd paled at the verbal assault, he couldn't stop.

'What are friends for but to share things? Do you think I'd have cared about my future—taken money from the man—if I'd known he was beating you? Dear God, Majella, did you think so little of me that you'd assume I'd put my future ahead of your welfare?'

She looked blankly at him, a look he now remembered from their childhood, and as her shoulders bowed he knew the last thing he should have done was shout at her. And though impotent rage—how could he not have seen? Guessed? Protected her?—still made him tremble, he put his arms around her and drew her close, whispering useless apologies for past and present, clasping her in his arms until the demands of their bodies changed the tenor of the embrace and they made love again, slowly and tenderly—sensibly this time—healing love...

Majella watched Flynn sleep, remembering the tenderness of his touch, the delight he'd brought her body, the sheer joy of making love with Flynn. Then she sighed and slid out of the bed, dressing easily as the light was still on. She looked at him again, seeing the angled planes of his face, the traces of silver in his black hair, the lips that had brought her such savage delight. With a little shiver that wasn't entirely remembered pleasure, she tiptoed around the bed, bent to kiss Flynn's cheek and turned out the light.

All she'd done, she realised as she drove back to the showgrounds through the still, moon-silvered night, was complicate matters. She sighed again. Maybe it was a good thing Parragulla House was beyond her reach finan-cially. Living here would be impossible. Making love to Flynn, with Flynn, had put an end to that dream, whichever way she looked at it. For a start, making love to Flynn had proved something she'd kind of suspected ever since they'd met again.

That she loved him…

So living near him, loving him, seeing him around the town would be unbearable, while having an affair with him—and that's all it would be, given his doubts about marriage—was beyond contemplation. Imagine Gracie going to school, the kids all talking about her mother and the doctor…

She crept into the cabin, touched her sleeping child on the cheek, then slipped into bed, wrapped her arms around herself and refused to cry.

Flynn woke to find her gone. Woke with so many twisted thoughts he didn't know where to start in sorting them out. The idea of the old man hitting his granddaughter was still hard to believe, but his subconscious had obviously accepted it, for the guilt Flynn felt that he hadn't known—hadn't protected her better—ate into him.

Concern about the consequences of unprotected sex flashed through his mind, of lesser importance for some reason—the thought of Majella being pregnant not as upsetting as it should be...

He chased away memories of the closeness they'd shared, knowing they were nothing but distractions, no matter how his body felt about repeating the exercise.

Soon.

Then there was the will and those damnable conditions. He hadn't finished telling her about the money—money that could make such a difference in her life, although now he knew what she'd suffered at the old man's hands, he could understand her reluctance to believe her grandfather might have meant well when he'd written it.

But before any of it could be hers, they had to get around the conditions.

Somehow.

An idea, as nebulous as a cloud at first, floated through his mind. His body caught on first, stirring again, remembering pleasure. Cold-shower time—think it through. How could he suggest it in such a way that Majella might accept the idea?

A friendly offer—nothing more. Explain to her how bad he felt that he hadn't been able to help her more when they'd been young—that he had been blind to that side of the old man…

Would that work?

It was all he had.

He pushed his body out of bed, showered and dressed. He had to talk to her, but where? Sophie and Helen would be in the cabin until the festival opened, and if Majella was working on the stall, talk would be impossible.

Here at his house wasn't all that good an idea either, given how 'talking' had ended the previous evening. They needed neutral ground.

An image of the gully popped into his mind. He'd phone the new shop in town that packed picnic baskets, order one for breakfast, then collect Majella and Grace and take them up by the creek. Spread a blanket on the violet leaves…

He found the cabin easily, mainly because Majella was sitting on the front steps, watching Grace play with stones around her feet. He pulled up in front of her and fancied he saw colour rise in her cheeks, but her eyes met his as he walked towards her.

'Man,' Grace called to him with delight, and it seemed natural to bend and lift the little girl into his arms.

'I've a picnic breakfast in the car,' he said, feeling Grace's arms tighten around his neck. 'You'll both join me?'

The pale eyes held a hundred questions, but sounds of movement in the cabin behind her must have helped Majella decide.

'I'll just tell Helen,' she said, and slipped inside, returning moments later with a jacket for Grace, and her car keys.

'Can we go in my car? It's got the booster seat.'

Tension was audible in the words and visible in the set of her shoulders, the slight tremor in her hands, and Flynn wanted nothing more than to put his arms around her and assure her that everything would be all right.

But who was he to give such reassurance?

A friend who'd already let her down...

While putting his arms around her wasn't such a good idea, recalling where a comforting hug had led last night.

With Grace secure on one arm he walked back to his car and reached in for the picnic basket, carrying it across to the small four-wheel-drive, setting the picnic basket on the ground while he put Grace into her booster seat.

Family day out—so domestic, Majella thought, watching the care with which Flynn handled her daughter.

A dream come true?

More a mirage, she reminded herself, wary of Flynn and confused about the new dynamics between them. She couldn't regret making love with him, for it had been too wonderful—too precious—for regrets, but it had made things more, not less, complicated.

Unless they both ignored what had happened.

Was that what he was doing? Opening the car door for her? Being careful not to touch her?

Her body ached for just a brush of fingers on her arm, or a breath of a kiss in her hair, for something, anything, that hinted of the bliss they'd shared, but no, today's Flynn was all cool remoteness.

She studied him as he moved around the car, opening the hatch to put the picnic basket inside. Was his face a little more set than usual? Did that show he, too, needed all his control not to reach out—to touch…

She parked where they'd parked when they'd searched the gully for the boys, and turned to Flynn, wanting a sign of—what?

No sign, so she asked.

'Why are we doing this?'

'We didn't finish the conversation about the will,' he said, and his face relaxed just enough for a hint of a smile to flit across his lips. 'I thought neutral territory, Gracie as chaperone, maybe we could sort things out.'

Could they?

Majella doubted it but she lifted Grace from her car seat and, carrying the little girl, followed Flynn up the gully to where the violets grew thickest. He spread a tartan blanket, then opened the bright basket, producing tubs of peeled and cut fruit, tiny pots of home-made yoghurt, croissants and pastries and little jars of jam and honey.

'Eat,' he ordered, offering an apple quarter to Grace, who sat herself down on the blanket near his feet and chewed happily on it. Then he opened a Thermos and the delicious scent of brewed coffee filled the crisp morning air.

'Bliss!' Majella said, breathing in the tempting aroma.

'Bliss indeed,' Flynn said, though a teasing glint in his eyes made her think he wasn't talking about the coffee.

She ate a little of this and a taste of that, enjoying the picnic, relaxing, but not entirely relaxed as she knew this was but a prelude.

'So, talk,' she said, when she'd finished a second cup of coffee, and Grace was happily picking leaves from a bush to feed to her toy koala.

'It's about the will—some other things,' Flynn said. He sounded so unlike Flynn—almost hesitant—that Majella laughed and said, 'I know it's not your fault he chose you as executor. And I know I got upset the first time you talked about it, but I promise not to yell at you this time. Just tell me what you have to tell me, so we can get the whole thing out of the way.'

Blue eyes scanned her face, as if trying to read her mood behind the brave words, then his hand reached out towards her, but he drew it back.

'Talk,' Flynn repeated, an order to himself to

get on with it, although his heart thudded with doubt. 'Last night you talked about a home— wanting a home for Grace.'

Majella nodded and he took a deep breath and plunged on.

'You can give her that—give her Parragulla House,' he said, the words sounding louder than he'd intended in the quiet glade beside the creek. Yet hesitant. 'One way out, I thought, would be for you to marry me. Not for real—well, it would have to be for real—but on a temporary basis. We like each other so we'd qualify as happy, and you'd be fulfilling the condition of the will. Then once everything's settled, we could get unmarried.'

Majella straightened on the blanket and stared at his face as if trying to process this unexpected suggestion.

Then she shook her head.

'You're like Helen,' she told him. 'You listen to me talk about independence and standing on my own two feet—making a life for myself and Grace—then you step right in and take it over, making it easy for me, finding answers for me. Jeff did that, too. I came into their house in much the same way as any other injured animal and he saw his role as taking care of me. And I let him, which was probably wrong, but I won't do that again. I don't want to be looked after, Flynn. It isn't what I need. Can't you see that?'

He shook his head, her refusal hurting although he hadn't really expected her to agree. But her stubbornness angered him as well, so, when she'd disentangled Grace from a vine and returned to the blanket with her daughter on her knee, he renewed his attack, bringing out the big guns in the argument.

'You're being stupid,' he growled, not loudly enough to upset the child who was rebandaging her koala's ear. 'It's a darned sight easier to be independent when you've got a million dollars plus in cold hard cash. All I'm suggesting is a temporary arrangement to see that you get what is yours by right anyway.'

Majella stared at him, unable to believe the figures he was flinging at her.

'A million dollars?' she whispered.

'More!' Flynn said, and Majella closed her eyes and tried to think.

Not easy, given the circumstances.

Had Flynn really just asked her to marry him?

That the proposal had come from Flynn her

childhood friend, not Flynn the lover from last night, she had no doubt. This was Flynn trying to make things right for her, especially now he knew about the scars. Flynn endeavouring to make up for the pain of her childhood.

So why was her heart leaping with excitement, thudding at her chest walls as if trying to escape its confinement?

And why was she thinking about a proposal she'd already turned down, and not the money?

She pressed her cheek to Grace's curly head and silently answered her own question, admitting the truth to herself.

Because to her Flynn was, and had been for a long time, more than just a friend. True, her love for him had been first love—a teenage adoration—but now they'd met again, she knew it was a love that hadn't ever gone away. Not completely! Neither had it been wiped out by her and Jeff's gentle, loving marriage. Apparently, it had been tucked out of sight, mostly forgotten, in a bottom corner of her heart, only reappearing—blossoming—slowly, shyly and uncertainly, now she and Flynn had met again.

Which was all the more reason not to take advantage of his offer, an offer made from kindness, or duty, or pity, or guilt.

Not love.

'A million dollars,' she repeated, so he'd think her mind had been considering the money all along, not floating off into dreams of love and marriage.

'More,' Flynn reiterated. 'Of course, there might be someone else in your life you'd prefer to marry in the next few weeks,' he added, although they'd gone way past the marriage part of the conversation, and even saying the words 'someone else' made him feel slightly ill.

Ignoring the side issues of his own internal feelings, he ploughed on.

'And if you don't want your grandfather's money for yourself, think about Grace. There's another million to be held in trust for her until she's twenty-five and more set aside for future children. Will you deny her that inheritance because you're too darned stubborn to bend a little?'

Majella lifted her head, opened her eyes and stared at him, her arms tightening around her child's small body at the same time.

'A million dollars for Grace when she turns

twenty-five?' she whispered, and he realised she wasn't worrying about or listening to his 'getting married' suggestions.

'With whatever interest that's accrued,' he explained.

'But that's terrible!' Majella said, losing Flynn completely.

'Terrible?'

'That much money given, just like that, to someone so young,' she muttered at him, awe and uncertainty colouring the words. 'It's—it's—irresponsible! She might get on drugs, go wild, anything could happen.'

'You're not that much older,' Flynn pointed out. 'If you were to get your grandfather's money, would you take to drugs? Go wild?'

'I'd use it for the rescue service,' Majella snapped at him. 'And for other charities. I have enough to live on, enough for both of us.'

'Then why assume Grace won't be as sensible and generous as you are? She's your child, Majella, and she'll have whatever beliefs and values you instil in her.'

Majella stared at him as if trying to take in what he was saying.

'But the temptation would be there,' she whispered, and he could hear her fear for the young woman she was picturing in her head.

'And you'd be there to guide her,' Flynn said gently, reaching out to take the leaves Grace was offering him. 'You, and Helen, and Sophie, and all the other people who come into her life in the next twenty-two years.'

Me?

He squelched the thought, knowing he, as both a friend and executor of the will, somehow had to help Majella make the decision that would be right for her and Grace.

She looked at him, her eyes pleading for something he wasn't sure he could supply.

'The house I want—money for the service—Grace's inheritance, all stacked up against a stupid desire on my part to stand on my own two feet!' A faint bitterness tinged the tired words, and strain showed around Majella's pale lips. 'Should I deny Grace that money for my own selfish reasons? Or because I fear for her stability when she's twenty-five? Of course I shouldn't!'

She half smiled, an expression so sad Flynn didn't want to look at it.

'You've even offered me a solution to the condition of the will. All I have to do is marry you, which would be the fulfilment of my girlhood dreams, and it's all mine. So why do I feel so unhappy?'

Flynn couldn't answer, his mind stilled by the 'fulfilment of my girlhood dreams' phrase.

But apparently she didn't need an answer, for she sighed and stood up, leaning down to tuck a corner of the blanket over Grace, who was lying down with the koala in her arms.

'I hope that's all you have to tell me,' Majella said, and he could hear the tiredness in her voice. 'I don't think I could absorb any more bizarre news right now.'

Flynn thought about the items on his mantelpiece at home and decided any mention of the letter and the little chest could wait. Majella looked exhausted—so pale he silently berated himself for not handling the situation more carefully.

He got up and put his arm around her shoulders.

'We'll work it out,' he promised her.

'Will we?' she asked, her voice so pitiful he turned her into his arms and held her in a comforting embrace.

A comforting embrace, that's all, he reminded himself, as excitement stirred, his senses remembering where another comforting embrace had led.

Majella leaned into him, finding comfort and something more in his arms, disturbed that her body wanted to remain there—that it was tempted by the warmth of the embrace. Sensations she shouldn't be feeling stirred in her breasts and tingled between her thighs.

Thoughts she shouldn't think—would a marriage of convenience be so bad when the man was Flynn? sneaked beneath her guard.

Would it hurt to say yes? To marry him? To find oblivion from the chaos in her mind in the pleasure she knew Flynn's body could provide?

'Of course it would,' she muttered, tearing her body out of that warm haven, no doubt startling Flynn with her cross words.

Although the way he was smiling, maybe he'd been following her thoughts.

'We'd be good together,' he said, then he kissed her gently on the lips, but not so gently the stirring didn't quicken and the tingling grow more intense.

'That's not the point,' she told him, stepping away before he could kiss her again.

Or she could kiss him!

'You've got to pack up the picnic things,' she reminded him, then walked away, taking Grace towards the creek, kneeling beside her while she splashed her hands in the water, showing her how small sticks floated on the water, playing with her daughter, her mind blocking out thoughts of money—thoughts of Flynn.

But as she drove back to the showground, she couldn't not think of the things he'd said—about them being good together, an innocent enough phrase but it had made her shiver with desire.

'I need to think,' she said, when she pulled up outside the cabin. 'About it all.'

'Including my offer of marriage?' he asked.

She looked at him, trying to read something in his eyes, but couldn't fathom just what lay behind this prompt.

Shook her head.

'I don't think that's an option, really,' she said sadly. 'A nice offer—a nice thought—but…'

'You'd marry someone else?'

His voice betrayed his disbelief. Or was it displeasure?

She shrugged.

'Surely it wouldn't be hard to find someone willing to marry me for a share of a million dollars.'

'Now you're being ridiculous!' he said crossly.

'You can't go marrying someone you don't know—he could take you for every cent of your inheritance, and what about Grace, have you thought of her? About the kind of influence some man you marry might have on her young life?'

'What kind of influence would *you* have, Flynn?' Majella shot back at him. 'Coming into her life on a temporary basis then leaving it again?'

Leaving it again? The idea filled Flynn with bleak despair. It was what he'd suggested but didn't Majella and her daughter deserve better than that?

'Let's talk tomorrow,' he said, touching her shoulder then opening the car door. 'Think it through, maybe talk to Helen. There's still time to decide which way you want to go. You could even get some legal advice about the conditions, although I've tried a number of solicitors and even asked for a barrister's ruling, and all agree the conditions can't be broken.'

He slid out of the car then leaned back in to touch a dozing Grace on the cheek, feeling a not entirely welcome delight when her eyes opened and she whispered, 'Man!' and smiled a sleepy smile.

CHAPTER NINE

BUT no amount of thinking seemed to help, Majella realised as she packed up some lunch for Grace and they made their way through the marquees to the Sherwoods' stall. Not that she could stop thinking about the things that Flynn had told her—and suggested—even while explaining a balm or telling someone about the rescue service. In the end, Helen suggested she take Grace for a walk, and though she enjoyed wandering down the main street of the town, pushing Grace in her stroller, stopping to let people admire her little girl, no solution to her problems magically appeared.

Although if she forgot about the will altogether, there was no problem. She could buy a house in some other small town, have runs built, and start a new sanctuary.

And if her heart ached at the thought, and the

friendly faces and welcoming smiles in Parragulla's main street tempted her, well that was just too bad.

Back at the cabin, she fed Grace her dinner, bathed the little girl and put her to bed.

'We're all going to the Chinese restaurant for dinner,' Sophie informed her, whirling into the cabin for a wrap then disappearing almost as quickly.

'I'm for an early night,' Majella told Helen, who'd followed more sedately. 'I'm bushed.'

Helen nodded, and departed, leaving Majella with her thoughts for company. Although, much to her surprise, once showered and tucked into bed, she didn't ponder on the pros and cons of money or marriage, but slept.

Slept well, and deeply until Grace woke in the early hours of the morning, fretful and grizzling quietly, so Majella took the little girl into her bed and sang soft nursery rhymes until she drifted off to sleep. But sleeping with the child was like sleeping with a—windmill?—as little arms and legs flailed around, and the small body tossed and turned.

By morning Grace was definitely feverish, her cheeks pink and her eyes glazed.

'She can't be teething,' the ever practical Helen told Majella, 'so it's probably just some bug she's picked up at the festival. Try some baby paracetamol and you stay here with her—you look as if you need a rest as well.'

Grace went back to sleep, but sleep evaded Majella, kept at bay by the echoes of Flynn's conversation and the things she hadn't thought about last night.

Flynn explaining there was money, Flynn suggesting she would be selfish to deny Grace a legacy, Flynn offering to marry her...

Her heartbeats accelerated just thinking of that moment, then sadness swamped the joy. He had offered out of kindness—in part to make up for her grandfather's behaviour, in part as the friend he'd always been. But how could she go into a pretend marriage with Flynn, feeling as she did about him?

It would be like living a lie...

Grace gave a cry then vomited, and Majella, lifting the wailing child into her arms, felt the heat in the little body and knew the paracetamol hadn't reduced her fever.

She bathed her gently, talking all the time, soothing the little one with words, but Grace's lack of response to the chatter was even more concerning than her temperature. Dressing her in nothing but a nappy, Majella held her on her knee, trying to persuade her to drink some water, wondering if she should phone the hospital— phone Flynn…

Flynn made his way towards the Sherwoods' stall for the fourth day in a row. He should probably have given Majella time to consider his solution to her problems, but impatience wouldn't let him stay away. He wouldn't pester her, he told himself, just check she was OK. Maybe take Grace to see the miniature animals that were always the main attraction on the Tuesday of the festival.

'She's not here.' Sophie stated the obvious as Flynn appeared. 'Grace was a bit upset this morning and Majella's stayed at the cabin with her.'

'Just a bit upset or sick?' Flynn demanded, then realised, from Sophie's startled look, that he'd been far too abrupt with his question.

Sophie shrugged.

'Mum would know but she's gone over to the fresh vegie market to get some stuff to take home. The cabin's down near the wood-chopping arena. Number seven—it's got a dark blue door. Oh, but you know that. Anyway, you could go and see them for yourself.'

Flynn thanked her and strode away, anxious to see Majella but a little anxious about Grace as well, although he knew full well that children could pick up an infection very easily then throw it off with equal ease.

He knocked on the blue door, and Majella called to him to come in, walking towards the door as he opened it. His eyes took in the worry in her expression, then Grace's hectically flushed cheeks.

'I was just considering whether to phone you or take her to the hospital. I know little ones can get sick very quickly and then better just as swiftly, but—'

'You should have phoned me straight away,' he said, smiling at Grace who offered him a weak effort in return but whimpered when he tried to take her from her mother's arms.

'Just rest her on the bed so I can look at her,' he said, but as Majella shifted the child in her arms he saw the purpura—red spots in the red flush on her left cheek.

'Better yet,' he said, 'let's get her to the

hospital. I can examine her more closely there—take some blood.'

He spoke casually, trying not to frighten Majella, although his own lungs had tightened and he felt as if a giant hand was squeezing at his heart.

'I'll put her in the car right now,' Majella said, and he saw the fear he'd tried to keep at bay, right there in her eyes.

'My car's way over near the entrance so I'll come with you,' he said, following her out and climbing into the back seat so he could be close to Grace. If it was meningitis, or its derivative meningococcal meningitis, she might convulse and if he were close…

Majella drove carefully, although Flynn guessed she'd have knocked aside anyone who strayed into her path.

'Meningococcal?'

She spoke the word he'd hoped she wouldn't guess as she pulled up at the hospital.

'There's a slight rash—it might be, or it might not,' he said, releasing Grace from the safety restraints of her booster seat and lifting her into his arms. 'I'll do tests right now and start treatment. I'll need to do a lumbar puncture for some spinal fluid. It's not a nice procedure but it's the only way we'll know for sure.'

Majella was following up the steps into the hospital—into A and E where they seemed to have spent an inordinate amount of time in the last few days.

'Treatment? You can treat it?'

'Of course,' he said, and turned to see two tears of relief trickle from her eyes.

A nurse appeared and he asked her to prepare a tray, explaining what he had to do.

He rested Grace on the examination table in the room where he'd treated Majella, talking reassuringly to the little girl all the time, although she was unresponsive, then he washed his hands and pulled on a coat and gloves, asking Majella to do the same.

'Mask as well, when we're ready,' he warned her. 'The danger of infection at the site is low, but we daren't risk it.

'We need her on her side with her knees curled up,' he explained to Majella, positioning Grace then asking Majella to hold her.

'There's a space between the fourth and fifth lumbar vertebrae,' he said, thinking an explanation of the procedure might distract Majella, even just a little. 'You slide the needle in, parallel to the table, angling it towards her belly button, then feel for the pop as the needle penetrates the protective sheath.'

Majella watched, anxiety for Grace making her feel detached from reality, although the fine needle penetrating Grace's skin had made her wince, and now she felt quite ill, as Flynn drew off three tubes of fluid.

'One for protein and glucose studies, one for cytologic and bacterial studies and one for cell count and serology,' Flynn explained, and Majella, although understanding the terms, worried only that so much fluid had been taken from her child's spine.

He taped a dressing in place, and lifted Grace so gently Majella thought her heart would break. Little girls should know the feel of a father's arms, she thought, then wondered fleetingly, as she sometimes did, about her own father.

'I'll settle her in a cot before I start a drip. I want to give her a dose of benzylpenicillin. If the test comes back negative for meningococcal it won't matter, and if it's positive at least we've been able to start treatment early.'

Once again, Majella followed him through the

hospital and into a small room furnished with a single bed. A nurse had followed them, carrying a tray with more paraphernalia on it, the covered needles making Majella shiver.

'There's a cot on the way,' Flynn said, as a rattling in the corridor suggested it was very close. 'I hate seeing little ones in a full-size bed—they look so small and lost it's frightening.'

A porter and a nurse entered the room and wheeled the bed away, replacing it with a small, blue-painted cot with sides that slid right down to allow the medical personnel easy access to the patient.

'Her cot at home is blue,' Majella said, and though she'd tried to sound matter-of-fact and, oh, so together, she'd heard the tremor in her voice and suspected Flynn had heard it, too.

But all he said was, 'That's good,' as he concentrated on getting a catheter into one of the tiny veins on the back of Grace's hand and taping it in place. He connected the fluid line, then spoke to the nurse who disappeared, returning with the small vial of the drug Flynn would introduce into the fluid flowing into Grace's blood.

The fact that the little girl remained so quiet throughout all this fussing told Majella just how ill she must be, and her knees grew weak as she considered, just momentarily, how serious the situation was.

'Sit there beside her. I'll send someone in with a cup of tea for you. Or would you prefer coffee?'

Majella stared blankly at him, unable to compute his words and make sense of the simple offer.

'Tea, I think,' Flynn said, touching her on the shoulder, giving it a reassuring squeeze. 'We found the boys,' he reminded her. 'And we'll get Gracie better.'

She looked into his eyes and saw the promise repeated there—the promise and something else. Something that looked a lot like love…

Shaking the fanciful notion away, she slipped into the chair Flynn had offered her and slid her hand through the cot to rest on Grace's leg.

'I have to go and phone the pathology service to make sure they rush the tests through,' Flynn said, reluctant to leave them but knowing he had to push the lab for results. 'But I'll be back. If it is meningococcal I'll need blood from you, Helen and Sophie for testing, to make sure you're not carrying the virus. Then you'll all need vaccinations.'

'You've been close to Grace, too,' Majella reminded him and he nodded but as he walked away he realised he'd been too close to Grace—not from the point of view of infection but because of how her illness was affecting him.

Majella was waiting anxiously when he returned, her car keys dangling from her fingers.

'My car—it's the only one we brought to Parragulla. A courier delivered all the products. Your car's still at the showground.' She offered him the keys. 'Would you mind taking mine back down and giving Helen the keys—letting her know what's happened?'

He checked the latest obs on Grace, then the drip feed and the catheter site and finally, when he could find no further excuse to linger, he took the keys and left the room, jiggling them in his hand.

Remote door opener? he wondered as he walked down the front steps. He looked more closely at the keys, sorting through them for the car key, seeing the identifying tab on the key ring, a plastic disc containing a photo. He'd had one made for his mother for Christmas, back when he'd been in high school—a photo of himself and his two sisters embedded in some type of plastic.

Thinking it might be a baby photo of Grace, he looked at it, and saw the blond man smiling at him.

Jeff?

It had to be.

A vague nausea churned in Flynn's stomach. Had he been subconsciously believing Majella hadn't cared for her dead husband, that the fact that she carried this constant memory of the man was so upsetting?

Or was it jealousy, pure and simple? An emotion he'd never thought to feel.

He found the car key, clicked open the doors, and drove down to town, returning the vehicle to the parking space outside the cabin and locking it, before walking back up to the marquees to give the keys to Helen.

Not looking at the photo!

Majella sat at Grace's bedside, willing the little girl to get better, but she was so unresponsive Majella had to fear the worst, although when Flynn returned he assured her this was normal and that Grace's body needed all its energy to fight off the virus.

Flynn sat with her whenever he could, made her eat and drink, told her stories about his days at university and reminded her of happy times they'd had together. Helen came mid-afternoon and later Sophie, but it was the times when Flynn was with her that Majella felt most at ease, not entirely because of his professional expertise.

Sophie arrived again at eight, announcing she was the first shift of the night, but her cheerfulness turned to tears when she saw how quietly Grace lay, and Majella had to comfort and reassure her young friend—then talk about the ball the following evening, diverting Sophie's mind successfully from Grace for a little while.

At midnight Helen arrived, handing the car keys to Sophie and telling her to drive carefully and make sure she got some sleep, and with Helen there, Majella felt secure enough to sleep herself, curled up on the folding bed a nurse had set up beside the cot.

She sensed more than heard a noise, and opened her eyes to see Flynn in quiet conversation with Helen at the door of Grace's room. Again car keys were exchanged, Flynn assuring Helen he could get a lift down to the showground to collect his car later.

Majella's first thought was for Grace, but a glance showed she seemed to be sleeping peacefully. Her second thought, inappropriately enough, was how much of a mess she must look. But apparently Flynn didn't notice, for he came and sat on the edge of the little bed and took her hand.

'Did you three have a roster of some kind worked out?' she asked him, so pleased to have him close she could have hugged him.

He smiled and nodded, and she gripped his fingers tightly.

'Thank you!' she managed, her voice husky with exhaustion. 'It wasn't until I was drifting off to sleep that I realised independence isn't all it's cracked up to be.'

'Then you'll marry me?' he teased, putting his arm around her shoulders and drawing her body to rest against his.

She leant against him, then found a tired smile.

'Ask me when it's for love, not for a house,' she told him, brushing a kiss against his ear lobe. 'But even independent women need friends.'

He tightened his arm around her shoulders, kissed her cheek, then stood up to take Grace's chart off the bottom of the cot and read the notes that had been made throughout the night.

'She's stable—which is a bland term that merely means her condition hasn't worsened during the night,' he said, not returning to the bed but settling in one of the two chairs by the cot. 'With meningococcal, which the lab's confirmed by email, it's mostly a matter of wait and see.'

He looked anxiously at Majella.

'Which means you have to take care of yourself so you can be there for her when she's getting better—that's when she's likely to be fractious and upset.'

So businesslike—doctoral—Majella thought, wanting, contrarily, for it to be the other Flynn, the one who'd held her in his arms and kissed the breath out of her, warming her body with urges she'd never felt before. The one who'd made love to her with such savage tenderness even with her baby sick her body reacted to his presence.

She ran her hands through her tousled hair and looked down at the grubby, rumpled clothes she'd put on the previous morning, probably still redolent of Grace's vomit, and realised it wasn't very likely he'd want to come within two feet of her, let alone hold her in his arms.

'Can you stay a little while?' she asked him.

'Long enough for me to have a shower? Helen brought some clothes…'

Had she sounded so uncertain that he stood up, came around the cot and, grasping one of her hands, pulled her to her feet? Then he took her in his arms, tousled hair, grubby clothes, baby sick and all, and held her close.

'Don't you know I'd stay for ever if I could?' he murmured, pressing kisses on her hair, her cheek, her nose. 'I can't, of course, I have to go to work later, and have other stuff happening today, but I'll be here for you when I can, and just a phone call away when I can't be with you.'

He didn't kiss her lips and fire the urges, but just being in his arms was bliss enough. Majella leant against him, feeding off his strength, wondering again about the independence thing.

A cough made them realise the nurse on duty had returned to take Grace's thirty-minute obs.

Majella broke away, feeling the heat of embarrassment, not desire. She grabbed the little overnight bag Helen had brought up, and hurried out of the room. She'd found a bathroom during the night and seen the shower stall, and now, as she stood under the steaming water, she felt confidence return.

As soon as Grace was better, and Grace *would* get better—they'd find a house to call their own. It didn't matter that it wasn't Parragulla House—it wasn't the house that made a home.

Refusing to think of any alternative, she dried herself and dressed, smoothing moisturiser into her skin and brushing the knots out of her hair before pulling it back, fastening it with an elastic band and securing it in a knot on top of her head.

'For someone who's only had a couple of hours' sleep, you don't look too bad,' she told herself, then felt a pang of guilt that she could be thinking of her appearance while Gracie was so ill.

'I do prefer it down,' Flynn said, when she walked back into the room, but the admiration in his eyes both belied the words and restored her confidence, which had begun to waver on the short walk from the bathroom to the cot.

'But you're a beautiful woman either way,' he added, almost to himself, before asking what she'd like for breakfast. 'You have to eat, Majella.'

Bossy Flynn again.

She settled on tea and toast, although when the tray arrived, it had fresh croissants instead of toast, and tiny pots of different jams to spread on them.

Flynn took the tray and set it on a table, then made her sit while he poured her tea and broke the croissants into moist, flaky pieces, spreading them with butter and jam, popping the first one into her mouth, his fingers brushing against her lips.

Majella felt her heart race at the touch and glanced guiltily towards Grace, lying white and still in the little cot, the rash startlingly red against her pale cheek now the fever had been reduced.

'Doing normal things like eating isn't hurting Grace,' Flynn said, reading her thoughts—or part of them—with ease. Then his phone buzzed in his pocket and he had to leave, squeezing her fingers and dropping a kiss on her head before he departed.

Majella picked up another piece of croissant, and chewed it thoughtfully. Of course it tasted the same as the one Flynn had fed her.

And of course he wouldn't be feeding her if they were married. It would be a matter of convenience, that's all—a temporary arrangement...

The thought made her heart ache.

CHAPTER TEN

GRACE was showing a definite improvement by late afternoon, so much so she ate a little stewed apple for her dinner then sat in the cot and played with Blinky, her toy koala, for a while.

Helen had brought up a lot of her toys, but the hospital staff had rigged up her greatest delight, a mobile of weird and wonderful hospital equipment tied to surgical thread—aluminium and stainless-steel objects that glinted and danced and jingled in the light breeze coming through the window.

It was out of reach but she'd worked out she could use Blinky to hit it, making the objects clang against each other.

She was doing this when Sophie came in to show off her finery for the ball.

'Oh, Sophie, you look beautiful,' Majella said,

taking in the carefully arranged blonde hair and the beautiful silvery blue dress.

Sophie coloured and spun around.

'Do you think so?' she said, wanting praise yet embarrassed by it.

'I do!'

'Pretty Sophie,' Grace offered, and though Sophie went to hug her, Majella held her back.

'Keep clear. Although we've all had the meningococcal vaccine now so there's no risk of infection, I'd stay clear of the lethal bear, which could be liberally smeared with stewed apple.'

Sophie laughed and ignored the warning, bending to kiss her little niece, then Helen arrived, looking very glamorous in a beautifully cut black dress.

'I hope you understand I have to go with Sophie,' she whispered to Majella. 'She's had her heart set on going, but there's no way she'd go on her own.'

'Of course you have to go,' Majella assured her, thinking rather wistfully of the dark red dress she'd bought especially for this ball. 'And make sure you have fun—that's an order.'

She saw them go, then tucked a sleepy Grace beneath the sheet and light blanket, and was contemplating a long lonely night when footsteps she now recognised echoed down the corridor.

Flynn, resplendent in a dinner suit and so handsome he took her breath away, entered the room.

To see his patient, of course—going to the cot and again reading through the latest notes.

'She's definitely on the mend,' he said to Majella, then he smiled, and looked even more devastating than he had when he'd walked in.

'Off to the ball?'

Good grief! What a lame thing to say! Talk about stating the obvious.

'I have to give a speech,' he explained, then must have read something in her face for he added, 'Feeling a bit like Cinderella, are you?'

'A bit,' Majella admitted, 'but there'll be other balls and there's no way I could enjoy myself, going off and leaving Gracie here.'

Flynn nodded and touched her lightly on the shoulder.

'I'll call in later,' he said, then he was gone.

Majella dozed in the chair, the lack of sleep the previous night, catching up with her. Then once again footsteps, lightly tapping sandals, and a heavier tread but not Flynn's, sounded in the corridor.

Sophie floated in, her cheeks flushed with wonder.

'This is Phil,' she said, dragging a reluctant young man into the room. 'He's just come to say hello, and I've come to say it was the best night of my life. Mum danced with about a hundred different men, Flynn was there, looking so dishy I nearly forgot about Phil, but the blonde on his arm gave me a dirty look when I said hello, so I kept clear, and then Phil's mate, Harry…'

Majella had stopped listening.

Flynn there with a blonde?

Does Rosemary know? The young man had said—the one who'd talked about the heiress.

Presumably Rosemary was blonde, and Flynn didn't have a string of women he was taking out…

Sophie stayed a little longer then she and Phil departed, explaining that Helen had gone home to bed but would be back very early in the morning.

Majella tried to sleep, but Sophie's words kept running through her head, so when Flynn appeared, still in his dinner suit but with his bow-tie dangling untied around his neck, she couldn't help but look for lipstick marks on his shirt, his cheek—his lips!

'Pleasant evening?'

Had he heard something in her voice that he stopped in mid-stride and looked at her?

'Very,' he said cautiously, continuing into the room to check on his sleeping patient.

'Did Rosemary enjoy it?'

Majella couldn't believe she'd said the words, but jealousy had tightened every sinew in her body and she couldn't have held them back for—well, for a million dollars.

'Ah!' Flynn said, coming to sit in the chair beside Majella's and reaching out to take her hand. 'It was an arrangement made a month or so ago. Rosemary is fairly new in town. She bought an old bank building with a very lucrative divorce settlement and has transformed the place, with bedrooms upstairs for B and B visitors and a great restaurant downstairs. Part of the yuppifying of Parragulla, I guess, but there are advantages in that we now have a couple of good restaurants in town.'

'And Rosemary?'

He knew exactly what she was asking, for he sighed, squeezed her fingers, then said, 'She and I have been out a few times. Nothing serious.'

'Does Rosemary know that?' Majella muttered, then waited for Flynn to answer her.

He didn't, but Majella couldn't let it alone.

'And if I'd said yes to your offer of marriage?' she asked, withdrawing her hand from his warm and tempting grasp. 'What would you have told Rosemary? Just hang in there for a couple of weeks—or however long divorces take—and I'll be free again? Or would you have kept dating her?'

Flynn stood up, sighed and ran his hand through his hair, messing up the tidiness but making him look so sexily rumpled that Majella's throat went dry and she wondered why she was baiting him.

'Majella, none of this is important,' he said, his barely controlled impatience biting into the words. 'Of course I wouldn't be seeing Rosemary if I was married to you, but you've not said one word in favour of that solution—you're more worried about being manipulated by your grandfather, or losing the independence you're so keen to achieve.'

'It's still not right,' Majella muttered, although she knew full well she was being contrary. 'Asking me to marry you and taking her to the ball!'

'You're talking nonsense because you're tired,' he snapped at her, then he walked away, out the door, his footsteps echoing again, but going in the wrong direction.

Grace was well enough to leave hospital the following day, and with the festival packed away for another year, they piled into the car and drove away.

Majella had tried to avoid Flynn since their confrontation in the early hours of that morning, although she had watched as he'd examined a lively, recovering Grace that morning, before discharging her.

'Make sure she doesn't overdo things for the next few days and if you're at all worried give me a call.'

He'd handed her a card, his fingers brushing against hers in the exchange.

'Call me anyway?' he'd added, the words not quite a plea but not as authoritative as Flynn's words usually were.

'I don't think so,' she'd said, and he'd scowled at her.

'We have to talk some time, Majella,' he'd said—stern *and* authoritative now. 'You can't just bury your head in the sand—the will has to be settled one way or another.'

'That's your job,' she'd said, lifting Grace into her arms and holding her close, denying all the urges she still felt to live in Parragulla House and make it ring with laughter.

There's more, Flynn should have said, and told her about the chest, but there were dark circles under her eyes from her sleepless nights and worry over Grace, and she'd lost weight during her vigil so looked too frail to be shouldering more problems.

The chest might not be a problem.

But the letter…

He said goodbye again, then, as he bent to kiss Grace's curls, she said, 'Man!' and reached for him, so he took her in his arms, feeling the weight she'd lost in the fragility of her bones beneath her skin, feeling his heart squeeze with anxiety for her, although he knew she was getting better.

'I'll carry her out to the car,' he said, and although Majella made to argue, he stalled her with a 'don't you dare' look as good as one of Belle's.

They drove away, Helen at the wheel, Sophie waving, Majella fussing over Grace, although he was sure she turned to look at him, and he imagined he could see the pale blur of her face still watching through the back window until the car disappeared from view.

He had to see her. For a start, there was the unprotected sex business—what if she was pregnant.

He ignored the tingle of excitement *that* thought caused.

Then there was the little chest, it and the letter, both things he had undertaken to hand over to her.

And on top of that, in all honesty, he had to see her because he missed her so badly he couldn't sleep, while his body ached for her in a way he'd never experienced before.

Certain they were the symptoms of flu coming on, he'd ignored the aching for a while, but the flu hadn't come and he'd been forced to think it might be something else.

Definitely not love-sickness—he was a doctor and knew that didn't exist.

But love itself, that was real. Unfortunately, there were so many kinds of love...

A quick search through the top of his dresser, where he emptied his pockets each evening, produced the Nature's Wonders card, with Helen

Sherwood's address and phone number. He considered phoning, then dismissed that idea, knowing it would be far too easy for Majella not to take the call.

The address was an hour's drive away, so he waited until the following weekend, then asked the doctor in the next town to take any emergency calls and, with the little chest safe on the passenger seat of his car, he set out.

He knew the road well, so it took little of his attention, which was a shame because it left him free to think.

To think about Majella.

To think about his feelings.

To think about a small girl-child who called him 'Man' and already held at least part of his heart in her tiny hand.

Could he be a father to another man's child?

Was that the issue?

Not really.

The issue was Majella.

How he felt about her…

Worse—how she felt about him…

Helen's house, he discovered, after driving—distracted?—past the turn-off four times, was set back in the trees on the edge of state forest, accessed by a dirt road which wound through the bush so it wasn't until you actually came upon the house that you realised someone was living there.

Too isolated for three women, was his first thought, while his second, on taking in the high wire fences and divided runs, was that at least he'd come to the right place.

He made his way along the fence, seeking a way in, then saw a double carport off to one side of the house, a door which would lead inside set into the side wall. In the run nearest him, a young dingo paced restlessly, back and forth, longing to be free, but no doubt held captive because of injury, for his left front paw was heavily bandaged, an old sock, thick with dust and grime, covering the bandage.

Beyond the dingo was a wider run with a couple of young wallabies hopping about, strewn straw at one end providing softness for their bedding.

Fascinated by this menagerie, he came closer to the dingo's fence, so he could peer further in. It seemed one of the wallabies had also been injured, bandages he hadn't noticed earlier because they were grey with dust around its chest.

Majella had been right in thinking the kennels

and dog runs at Parragulla House would be ideal for this type of work.

He walked on to the door, his anxiety about seeing Majella again all but forgotten in the intrigue he felt about the animals.

'Hi, Sophie. I wanted to check on Grace, and I have something to give Majella. Is she here?' he said, when Sophie, clutching a tiny, furless baby koala to her chest, answered the door, Grace peering out from behind her legs.

'Man!' Grace said, with obvious delight, holding up her arms and confident of his reaction.

He swung her up, nuzzling kisses into her neck, delighting in the gurgling laughter of her response. He was happy to feel a little more flesh on her bones than had been there when she'd left hospital.

He could love her, that's for sure...

'She's hopeless,' Sophie said, slipping the tiny koala into a pouch made out of a padded kitchen glove. 'Man mad. You should see the fuss she makes of Phil.'

Flynn ignored the stab of jealousy this statement caused, and cuddled Grace closer, blowing her soft curls while she chortled with delight.

'Majella's operating,' Sophie said. 'Come and see.'

She led Flynn through the house, past bags hung on chairs, with lumpy marsupials pouched inside, and a galah with a broken wing, screeching from a cage.

'Operating?' he repeated, but right then Sophie opened a door, took a protesting Grace from his arms and waved him inside.

It had been a bathroom originally, he guessed. One of those big, old-fashioned bathrooms. The bath and toilet suite had been removed, but taps remained, big sinks fitted under them and stainless-steel benches, shelving and cupboards built around the walls

And Majella was indeed operating. Her patient appeared to be a wombat—a large hump of unconscious animal on a stainless-steel trolley. Majella stood on one side, scalpel in hand, while Helen, clad like Majella in a gown, mask and cap, appeared to be the theatre nurse, passing instruments and swabs.

'Appendicitis?' Flynn suggested, as Majella's pale eyes, seeming larger when they were all that was visible between the coverings, met his.

'Barbed wire,' she responded calmly, though he thought he saw a trace of panic in her eyes. 'Must have been an old fence, the wire trailing on the ground. He got caught up then made things worse trying to untangle himself. His mouth's a mess as well, as if he's tried to bite it off.'

She offered this explanation as if it was perfectly normal for her—or anyone—to be removing barbed wire from the nether regions of a wombat, but for all its practicality it didn't help Flynn one little bit.

Helen, who'd turned to see who had entered, must have sensed his confusion.

'Majella did tell you we take in injured wildlife?'

Flynn nodded, remembering the poster and various conversations, but still bemused to see the pair of them at work.

'There are people doing this all over Victoria,' Helen added. 'All over Australia actually. We have some vets on side who let us stand in on operations they do and provide some basic training. We need to do more training in a sanctuary to get permission to have drugs in the house, and, of course, we need to keep the drugs secure. We can't save every animal that comes our way, but we can help a lot of them.'

She turned back as Majella asked for a swab, and that was it as far as the explanations went.

Majella's attention remained fully on the wombat as she stitched up the wound she'd made when removing the treacherous wire. Stitched it up with what looked like fishing line.

'It is,' Helen said, when he queried it. 'We need something really tough because you know how itchy healing wounds can get and you can't tell a wombat not to scratch.'

She handed Majella a jar of salve, and as he watched her smear it over the wound and add a little more around the wombat's face, Helen smiled at him.

'Not Hakea Teritifolia,' she teased, 'but a salve mixed with the essence of the wild dog rose. It's not only good for healing native animals, but it helps them overcome their fear of humans while they're being nursed.'

His disbelief must have been written all over his face, for he saw the smile in Majella's eyes—enough of a smile for him to wonder if perhaps things might be all right between them.

Eventually…

While Helen cleaned up, he helped Majella lift the wombat off the table onto a small, low trolley, then waited while she wheeled it away, presumably to somewhere it could sleep off the anaesthetic.

Helen stripped off her theatre gear, washed her hands, then led the way back to the kitchen, where Sophie was now feeding a larger animal, while Grace held a feeding bottle to the leather lips of her toy koala.

'Coffee?' Helen asked, and when Flynn said yes, Sophie reminded her mother they had an appointment in town.

'I was remembering. Majella will get the coffee when she comes back,' Helen said, studying Flynn as if she might somehow read the reason for his sudden appearance in his face.

Helen left, saying something about showering and getting ready, passing Majella in the doorway.

'Are you allowed to do this? Keep wild animals?' Flynn asked, half his mind on the strange new world in which he found himself, the other half on Majella, who was wearing unremarkable jeans and a T-shirt yet looked so good to him he could feel his body stirring with a desire so strong he wondered if she could feel it.

'Only with innumerable permits and regulatory agreements, and we can only keep them until they're cured. We have a vet who works with all the local wildlife refuges, operating on koalas with Chlamydia psitacci—have you heard of it? It's causing blindness in koalas right across Australia but an operation can cure it. We have a special permit for keeping them, post-op, as well.'

Flynn shook his head, answering her question about the disease, but also in disbelief that he knew so little about the native animals of his own country. He was about to ask for more information about the disease, when Sophie said, 'Peter, he's the vet, is wonderful. He's gorgeous too and totally in love with Majella although she's always refused to go out with him, first saying it was too soon after Jeff, then using Gracie as an excuse, or being in the army and not knowing where she'd be next week so it was no use starting something when they couldn't keep on seeing each other.'

Short pause during which Flynn wondered if both the women in the room would realise how tense his body had grown, because the tension seemed to be spreading from him and into the air around him.

'Of course,' Sophie continued blithely—obviously she felt nothing at all—'now Majella's been demobbed or whatever it's called, she can say yes next time he calls.'

Flynn looked at the woman whose social life Sophie was arranging, hoping to see a look of distaste on her face, or hear an objection from her lips. But she was looking at Sophie, not at him, a little frown on her face.

Wondering if she *would* go out with Peter the wonder-vet next time he asked?

Then Helen returned.

'I told Flynn you'd do coffee,' she said to Majella. 'Sophie, I'm leaving in ten minutes if you want to change.'

She left again, Sophie tucking the tiny joey she'd been feeding back into a pouch, before following her out of the room.

'Tact?' Flynn asked, following Majella to the sink where she filled a kettle then put it on to boil.

'I'm assuming she thinks you've come for a reason and it isn't to see her or Soph. Although she does have an appointment in town later today,' Majella said, turning towards him, her hips resting against the bench, so close he could lean in a little and their lips would meet.

Or would if he didn't have Grace sitting on his foot, talking to her toy, telling it she'd get some gum leaves for it, because it was too old for milk.

'I did need to see you,' he said instead of kissing Majella, not certain kissing was a good idea right now. Kissing tended to make everything far more complicated, although during the kiss everything seemed so right.

'We could, of course, spend the rest of our lives joined at the lips,' he muttered. He only realised he'd spoken aloud when he heard Majella's loud, 'What?'

'I was thinking that everything seems right between us when we're kissing—kissing or making love—but wrong the rest of the time,' he explained, still muttering because he was sure this was more girl talk than manly conversation!

Which was possibly why he was so thoroughly mixed up.

Majella had given up all pretence of making coffee and was staring at him.

'Is that what you came to tell me—that we're OK when we're kissing or making love?'

'Of course not,' he snapped, but he couldn't think for the life of him what he had come to talk about, his mind blocked by memories of their love-making.

'Well, if you came to talk about the will again, don't bother,' she said. 'There's no way that old man is going to force me into a marriage neither of us want. I've got enough security for me and Grace. We'll manage. The Parragulla House idea was probably stupid anyway. Some kind of hangover from the past—unfinished business. After all, I never felt my mother's presence in it when I was a child, so why, just because I'm a mother now, would she be there for me?'

He remembered her talking about her mother and the house and somehow this denial hurt him more than anything she'd said before.

But it also reminded him of why he'd come.

'It's not about the will,' he said. 'There's something else. Your grandfather left a letter and a little chest. Not long before he died, he asked me to find you and give them to you.'

'A letter? From him?'

She spoke in much the same way someone might say, 'A bomb? A live one?'

Flynn shrugged.

'It won't be much,' he warned her. 'He was

paralysed. He could move his left hand just a little and managed to write a little bit with that, so I doubt it would be a ten-page apology for his behaviour towards you.'

Majella smiled.

'Or a half-page apology. He wasn't one for apologies. Mainly, I guess, because he was always so certain he was right.'

'They're in the car,' Flynn said, then Grace diverted both of them, demanding lunch.

Flynn lifted her into his arms and held her while Majella made a sandwich, then cut up little sticks of cheese, carrot and apple and put them on the plate beside the bread.

'High chair over there,' she said to Flynn, who carried Grace across and settled her in her chair, fitting the safety restraints around her little chest, finding a certain sense of satisfaction that he could do these things for Grace.

'Hands and face,' Majella said, and Grace, babbling happily in anticipation of her lunch, held out her hands then held her face up to be wiped by the small washcloth.

'Will she eat all of that?' Flynn asked, as Majella put the plate and a small, lidded mug of milk on the high-chair tray.

'And ask for more some days,' Majella said, smiling proudly at her daughter, so pleased her appetite had returned.

Now she made the coffee, thinking of the chest and letter Flynn had in the car, feeling the same apprehension she felt when she treated an injured snake.

'Grace will have a sleep straight after lunch,' she told Flynn, knowing he'd understand she wanted to wait until the child was safely tucked in bed before she faced whatever emotional storm the chest and letter might blow her way.

She took a deep breath and forced herself to think of the present, not the past or the future. The present meant settling Gracie down for her sleep. Majella lifted her car keys off a hook near the kitchen door and tossed them to Flynn.

'If you're going out to your car for this chest you have to give me, would you mind bringing in Grace's blanket? It's a tattered blue object with a couple of bits of satin ribbon still intact around the edges. It's probably in her booster seat.'

'Security blanket?' Flynn asked, knowing most children had something they liked to hold as they slept.

Majella nodded, and smiled, making him think

that, as an adult, what he'd really like to hold as he slept was—

He cut off the thought and went out to the cars, opening Majella's first, noticing, as he fiddled through the keys for the one to open the car, that the tag—and photo—were gone.

Weird sensations riffled through his body. Sadness for the man who'd died, yet some kind of relief as well—even a sneaky squib of hope…

He set them all aside, got the blanket and the chest and letter, and returned to the kitchen.

Grace was in bed, and the letter and chest sat unopened on the kitchen table. Majella could only stare at them, wondering what new surprises—or what new pain—might lie in store for her.

Eventually, she lifted the little chest and felt its weight—not heavy—then looked at the clasp on it and for the first time realised there was a tiny padlock on it. A locked padlock.

Now she picked up the letter and felt its contents. Paper rustled within it but in one corner her fingers made out the outline of a key.

'There's a key for this in the letter,' she said to Flynn as he joined her by the table. She showed him the padlock then realised that if he'd had the chest for the months since her grandfather's death then he would already know that.

'So, letter first,' he said gently. 'You don't have to read it if you'd prefer not to.'

Majella felt her stomach turn, and a vague nausea made her press her hand to her lips, but she breathed deeply and handed the letter to Flynn.

'Open it,' she said, then saw a slight tremor in his hands as he slit the top of the envelope with a knife off the table and tipped out the letter and the tiny brass key.

The letter appeared to be one single sheet of paper, and whatever was on it wasn't good from the way Flynn frowned at it. In fact, the dark fury on his face made her shiver.

'What?' she whispered.

'That bastard! That bloody bastard. No "I'm sorry", no attempt to make amends. Everyone was right in their opinion of him—he was an arrogant, selfish old bully. Honestly, Majella, how you turned out so great with even a little of his blood in your veins is a miracle.'

He flung the letter down on the table, but when she reached out to pick it up he grabbed it out of her hands.

'It says nothing,' Flynn told her. 'Not a damn thing except that the chest was left for you by your mother.'

He crumpled the letter in his hands, and though Majella believed that was all that was in it, she couldn't understand why Flynn was so upset.

'That can't be all,' she said, and he came and wrapped his arms around her.

'It is, sweetheart. Not another bloody thing.'

Majella felt the warmth of Flynn's arms around her, and relished the sense of security they gave her, but she had no idea of where she stood with Flynn. That they were friends again she was nearly sure, but more than that?

Not a clue! She was too inexperienced—Jeff had been her only boyfriend—so way out of her depth as far as relationships went! And the reunion with Flynn had been so muddled—anger and re-criminations and love-making all in the mix..

She eased out of his arms—too easy while within them to think in terms of something more than friendship—and picked up the key.

'If it *is* from your mother, it won't contain anything to hurt you,' Flynn told her, picking up the chest then urging her to sit down before she opened it.

Which was all very sensible until Majella felt the key in her hand and realised her mother's hands had held it just like this. Her mother's fingers had touched the object she was touching now. And the mother she had never known had snapped the padlock shut—on what?

Her own dreams?

A treasure for the daughter she'd never see grow up?

Had she known that as she'd closed the chest?

Majella fiddled with the key, fingers shaking now, and looked to Flynn for help.

'Do you want me to do it?' he asked, so gently she felt tears prick at her eyelids.

'No, I can manage,' she whispered, not wanting to do it but not wanting him to do it either—to touch the key…

She unlocked the tiny mechanism and removed it from the hasp, setting it down on the table, her fingers lingering over it as if touching it was somehow connecting her to her mother.

She lifted the lid of the chest very carefully, pushing it back as far as it would go so Flynn, too, could see the slightly yellowed garments packed inside it. But right on the top was another letter, the name 'Majella' printed in block letters across the front of it.

'It's not Grandfather's writing,' Majella whispered, smoothing her fingers across the name, her voice so husky with unshed tears it took considerable resolve for Flynn not to lift her into his arms and hold her while she looked at it.

Darn it all! Why not? This was Majella—his friend.

He stood up, pushed the chest back from the edge of the table, then bent and lifted her into his arms, ignoring her protests.

'You can sit on my knee and I'll hold you while you read it,' he said. 'That way if you need a hug I'll be ready.'

She turned to him and he saw two fat tears leak from her eyes and dribble down across the freckles.

'You think I'll need one, do you?' she said, choking out the words.

'I'm damn sure you will, and if you don't then I will. This emotional stuff gets to me as well, you know.'

'What a girl!' she teased weakly, proof that his decision to hold her was making her feel better able to cope. But she didn't reach out for the chest again, or open the letter she held in her hand, snuggling into him instead, which wasn't particularly good for his resolve.

Or his libido!

CHAPTER ELEVEN

'GIVE me the letter,' he said. 'I'll read it to you.'

She handed him the letter and turned so she could watch his face as he read it.

Flynn opened it carefully, pulling open the old seal, then unfolding the two sheets of paper, lifting the top one to check the bottom of the second page.

'Mary Elizabeth Goldsworth,' he said, reading out the signature. 'Your mother's name?'

Majella's smile was forced.

'I only know that because the teachers at the school often called me Mary Elizabeth, mistaking me for my mother. Grandfather always called her "your mother" as if actually pronouncing her name might burn his mouth or sentence him to eternal damnation or something.'

Flynn wrapped his arms around the woman

on his lap and hugged her tightly, nuzzling his lips into her hair so she wouldn't notice his eyes had gone misty at this information and call him a girl again.

'If you don't want to read it, I will,' she said, just in time to stop Flynn's body getting over-excited enough to take the nuzzling further.

'No, I'll do it,' he said, removing his arms and returning his attention to the letter.

He read it silently, shaking his head all the while, slipping the first page behind the second while he took in the rest of it, before carefully folding it and setting it down on the table.

Then he swallowed the enormous lump that had swelled in his throat, took Majella's face between the palms of his hands and kissed her on the lips.

'I can't read it to you,' he said, 'because I'd howl like a baby while I did it and you wouldn't understand a word of it, but the gist of it is—' He paused and kissed the softness of her lips once again. 'Your mother found out too late that she had a problem with her pregnancy and that it was probably genetic. She doesn't say what it was but pre-eclampsia and eclampsia are the most likely, I would say. They aren't genetic but can be familial, although these days—even twenty-seven years ago—they can be managed. Women don't have to die from these conditions.'

'We have to remember she was only fifteen— maybe sixteen—little more than a kid. What did she know about pregnancy?' Majella whispered.

Flynn nodded his agreement, his mind off medicine now and back on the contents of the letter.

'Anyway, the doctor she must eventually have seen apparently told her that not only might she die but that you might also not survive. But if you did, she said, she wanted you to be named Majella—she must have had an amniocentesis and known you were a girl—after a guy called Gerard Majella, who, she says, is the patron saint of difficult births and mothers and various other family folk in trouble. Because, your mother said, your living would mean he'd listened to her prayers.'

Too choked up to continue, Flynn drew Majella close again, cuddling her against his body, holding her while she, too, spent some grief through tears.

Eventually she drew away again, but the tear stains on her cheeks proved his undoing and he had to find his handkerchief—no easy feat with a woman on his lap—and dry them all away. Then he had to kiss her once again, before he got back to the story.

Tender, gentle kisses—loving kisses…

'She also apologises for leaving you with only your grandfather to bring you up. As well she might, considering how he treated you,' Flynn muttered, but this time Majella stopped *his* lips with a kiss.

'He didn't hit my mother, so she wouldn't have known,' she whispered. 'I know because he always said, even as he beat me, that with her he'd spared the rod and spoiled the child and he wasn't going to make the same mistake twice.'

Flynn could only hold her tight against his body, unable to speak for the pain that ricocheted through him—for the huge lump in his throat.

So it took Majella's quiet prompt, 'Go on,' for him to pick up the letter again, this time reading directly from it.

'She says you should understand that he is driven by this one rule, "doing the right thing", but the problem is his heart died with my mother, your grandmother. If he ever had a heart! So love will never be allowed to cloud what he sees as his duty.' And she finishes, "I am sorry, Majella, but he's all there is left to look after you. With any luck he'll give you to an adoption agency and you'll end up with normal parents but if not, be brave and hang in there. At least you'll have the horses. He always let me ride— it was the only thing he ever encouraged me to do. I love the horses—they are my friends. Them and Bill. I hope he hasn't sacked Bill for giving me the money to get away. I hoped by running away he need never know about you, but now I've mucked things up because I'm probably going to die and leave a baby behind. I hope I leave a baby behind." And she says goodbye.'

Majella took a deep breath to stem further tears before they fell, then she rubbed her fingers across the pages of the letter, touching paper, but touching her mother as well.

'Old Bill helped her. I'm sorry I didn't know that,' she whispered. 'He might have helped me, too.'

'I would have helped you,' Flynn told her. 'I get so angry thinking of what your grandfather did to you, then even angrier with you for not saying anything.'

She turned on his lap and took his face

between the palms of her hands, holding it as he had held hers earlier.

'You were the last person I could tell, Flynn,' she said, and she leant forward and kissed him on the lips. 'Do you know why I ran away?'

'Because your grandfather beat you?' Flynn offered.

'He'd been doing that for as long as I could remember,' she muttered, straightening up and touching the scar by her eye. 'But that night—that was different. Do you remember where I'd been that night?'

'Majella,' Flynn said, feeling the tension in her body as he wrapped his arms around her. 'Sweetheart, we didn't even know you'd gone—let alone that you'd run away. I saw you at the stables one night, we'd arranged to ride the following day, you didn't come, then a couple of days later there's your grandfather telling me to put your riding tack away. As I told you earlier, he said you'd decided to go back to school because some of your friends were returning early. Naturally I believed him.'

'Believed I'd go back to school without saying goodbye to you? After you'd kissed me? After I'd told you I loved you?'

Flynn shook his head.

'You were fifteen, love. My sisters were in love with someone different every week. And it never occurred to me that he might tell a lie. I mean, why would he?'

'Because I'd run away,' Majella whispered, in a voice that suggested she'd expected more of him.

Or had expected more of the youth he'd been...

'But I didn't know that—none of us did. So, tell me, what happened?'

'He caught me that night when I came back to the house after sneaking out to meet you at the stables. He wanted to know where I'd been and who I'd been with and when I wouldn't tell him, he hit me across the face for the first time ever and said he'd beat it out of me.'

'You should have told him you'd been meeting me,' Flynn managed to say, while his mind rattled through all the ramifications of this new knowledge, and useless fury built inside him. 'Why did you make him angrier by not telling him?'

Majella lifted her head to look into his eyes, giving him a funny little smile.

'How could I tell him when I knew what it would mean?'

'The money for me to go to university!' Flynn said bitterly. 'I can't believe you let that count. Do you think I'd have minded, if I'd known? Do you think I'd have taken his money if I'd even suspected how he treated you?'

She kissed him again, gently cutting off his anger.

'Of course you wouldn't have minded, neither would you have taken his money—that's why I *had* to go, Flynn. I didn't care what he did to me, but if he'd hurt you—killed your dream of becoming a doctor—I couldn't have stood that.'

Flynn tightened his arms around her body and rocked her on his knee, trying to absorb all that he'd just learnt—the knowledge that it had been he who had prompted Majella's flight eating into him like a cancer.

'Look!'

He fought his inner demons, turning to see what Majella held.

A tiny dress, once white but now cream with age, and bootees and a bonnet, each one lifted carefully out of the little chest and set on the table.

'She must have loved me, mustn't she?' she whispered, as she ran her fingers over the little garments. 'To have got these things ready?'

Three small singlets, all embroidered, rather unevenly, with pink rosebuds, joined the other clothes on the table, Majella's fingers trembling now as she unpacked this unexpected treasure. Then, right at the bottom of the chest, she found a small, leather-bound book.

'You'll have to lift it out,' she said to Flynn. 'My hands are shaking too much.'

He reached around her and pulled it out, then set it on the table, opening the cover—not a book but a photo folder, on one side a photo of a young girl so like Majella it had to be her mother, and on the other side a photo of a young man— barely more than a boy—dark haired and dark eyed—unidentified but presumably Majella's father.

'Parents—I've got parents,' Majella whispered, and Flynn realised she was close to breaking point, the emotion of the chest's revelations almost too much to bear.

A demanding yell from some back room prevented any further explanation, and as Majella went to rescue Grace from her cot, Flynn studied the photos. Would photos help Majella feel closer to her parents? Would they go at least some way towards making up for all she'd lost in her youth?

Flynn hoped so and with the hope came a determination to make up to her himself.

Not that he could suggest such a thing to her—not to a woman determined to prove her independence.

Grace's presence prevented further discussion although Majella did make the coffee promised earlier and they sat outside at a table beneath the gum trees, Grace feeding grass through the fence to a young wallaby, Flynn asking Majella more about the rescue service, learning about similar services operated overseas—but mainly learning more about this adult Majella, who spoke so passionately about her work, who bent so wonderingly over the treasures her little daughter, now bored with the wallaby, found and brought for her inspection.

'Stone,' she said to Grace, when she plopped a polished pebble on the table. 'What colour is it?'

'Red!' Grace announced, so proudly Flynn couldn't have corrected her.

But Majella had no such inhibitions. 'I think it's more like brown, pet,' she said easily, and Grace repeated the word a couple of times then went off again.

'She looks well,' Flynn said, and Majella's eyes shone as she turned towards him.

'She does, doesn't she? I keep reading of children who've been really sick with that disease who've lost limbs or parts of limbs. Worst of all was that I should have had her vaccinated against it, but I was away when she was old enough, then somehow it just got pushed aside.'

Flynn took her hand across the table.

'We can't vaccinate kids against everything that might happen to them in their lives,' he reminded her. 'Much as we might wish we could.'

Majella smiled at him. This was so easy and natural, sitting here with Flynn, Grace playing at their feet. They could almost be a family.

'I've got someone covering for me tonight,' Flynn said, interrupting a pleasant little daydream she was having about a family. 'Would you be free for dinner? There's a new place not far down the road—a new B and B that has a restaurant attached. I thought I might book in there for the night. We could have dinner and I could come back and see you again tomorrow.'

'Why?'

He frowned at her.

'Why what?'

'Why come back and see me in the morning? You've given me the things Grandfather left. Was there something else?'

He tried to smile but the effort was so pitiful she felt her heart flinch.

'Wanting to see you again?' he said. 'Is that not enough of a reason?'

Majella would have loved to ask why again, but something held her back.

Although if they were having dinner…

'If we're having dinner?'

This time Flynn's smile was far more healthy.

'OK,' he said. 'I give in.'

He held up his arms in surrender, and Grace, catching the gesture, thought it meant something different and came over to scramble onto his knee.

He put his arms around her, relishing her warmth, and looked at Majella over Grace's head.

'I want to see you at dinner, and again tomorrow, and in whatever free time you and I might be able to manage together—possibly for the rest of our lives?'

Majella stared at him, trying to process the words, repeating the last phrase in helpless confusion.

'Rest of our lives?'

His answer was a smile like none she'd seen before—a smile that teased and tempted, was full of hope, yet held a little dread in it as well. Gracie was squirming on his knee, turning to pat his cheek and clutch his ear, but though his arms encircled her to keep her safe, his blue eyes never left Majella's face, the same hope and dread she'd read in the smile lingering in them.

'I thought, if you agreed, we could get married on the second of October?'

'You've lost me!' she said, dragging her thoughts away from love and hopeful eyes. 'Get married? Second of October? We haven't been to dinner yet!'

'I've blown it, haven't I?' Flynn muttered. 'Honest to goodness, I was going to do this properly—to ask you tonight—to go down on bended knee and all. I'd even thought I might have time to buy a ring this afternoon, but then thought it was better if you chose.'

Majella was staring at him as if he was a total stranger and no wonder, he was babbling—had lost the plot completely.

'Why?' she said again, and Flynn's mind scrabbled for a reason for the why.

His blowing it?

Surely not.

'Why were you going to ask?'

'Why was I going to ask?' Addled, that's what he was, though now Grace had scrambled off his knee, things might be easier. 'Why was I going to ask you to marry me?'

Majella nodded.

'Because you said to,' Flynn told her. 'That morning at the hospital. You said to ask you for love, not for a house. And if we get married on the second of October, the day after the deadline, then you'll know for sure it's not for the house. We'll get a few acres somewhere just out of town, and build the runs you need, and I can help you with the operations, maybe even learn to do the ops on the koala's eyes.'

She could feel excitement shimmering through her body, and ached to throw herself into his arms, but she wasn't quite there yet.

'I know it's becoming a little repetitive,' she said, teasing him gently, 'but again I have to ask why.'

'Why?' Grace repeated the word and this time climbed onto Majella's knee.

He didn't answer for a very long time, then before he did, he reached across the table and took her hand.

'Because I love you,' he whispered. 'Surely you must know that, although it took me far too long to work out that the panic I felt when I saw you crawl into that cave, and the pain I felt when Gracie was so sick, and the sleepless nights I've suffered since you went away all added up to love.'

Majella squeezed his fingers.

'It doesn't sound very comfortable,' she said, smiling at him, hoping all the love she felt was shining in her eyes.

'It's not,' he said, 'although it could be eased if you'd just say something other than "Why?"'

'Like what?' She squeezed his fingers. 'Like "I love you, Flynn"? Would that do?'

Flynn felt as if his heart would burst, yet suddenly it all seemed too easy.

'You're sure?' he asked, and Majella set Grace down on the ground, pulled up a tuft of grass and gave it to the little girl to feed the wallaby.

'Would this convince you?' she said, coming around the table and reaching out her hand to Flynn, drawing him to his feet, then stepping into his arms, folding his body close to hers, before kissing him full on the lips.

It began as a confirmation of her love but turned into something very different. It scorched its way through her body, making it throb in places she doubted had ever felt sensation. She pressed her pelvis forward, wanting to feel him against her, while her heart raced and her nerves tingled and the little hairs on her arms stood to attention.

'Flynn!' she murmured, not knowing words to tell him what she felt.

'Hush!' he whispered, letting his mouth tell her what she needed to know, accepting this silent confirmation of her love.

Then Grace was there, wedging her little body between their legs, demanding attention from one of them. Majella responded first, lifting her daughter into her arms and looking at Flynn with new questions in her eyes.

'There's Grace,' she reminded him quietly.

'Do you think I haven't considered her?' he said, reaching out to tweak one of Grace's curls. 'Haven't wondered if I can be a father to her—do right by her? Loving her is easy, but the rest? I'll try, Majella, that I promise you. I know she's Jeff's daughter, just as I know Jeff will always own a little piece of your heart, but I'll do my utmost to be the best replacement father she could have.'

Majella smiled at him over Grace's head.

'Loving her will be enough,' she said, then turned as a car drove into the yard.

'Dinner?' Flynn asked, and Majella nodded.

'I'll pick you up,' he said. 'Eight?'

She nodded again, too full of love and hope and joy to speak, hugging Grace so tightly the little girl squirmed in her arms.

He brushed a kiss across both their heads then left.

'You going?' Helen said when he passed her in the carport.

'Just up the road. I'll book in at that B and B, and come back to take Majella out to dinner. Is that all right with you? Do you mind babysitting yet again?'

Helen looked from him to Majella, who'd followed him more slowly through the house.

'I don't mind at all,' Helen told him, then she smiled. 'Especially as it looks as if this might be a special occasion.'

Then she turned back to Flynn.

'But you don't have to book in down the road. We've a guest bedroom.'

She didn't add, 'Or you could share Majella's room,' although there was a speculative gleam in her eyes.

Would he?

He glanced at Majella and knew the answer immediately. This was her home but it was also her mother-in-law's house. There's no way she'd share a bed with Flynn under this roof.

But...

'Well, if you don't mind,' he said to Helen. She assured him they'd be happy to have him, adding, 'Go get your things and I'll show you the room and where the bathroom is, and basic directions so you don't get lost. The place rambles a bit.'

He got his overnight bag, then followed Helen into a room that was bright and airy, furnished with a three-quarter bed, bedside table, a comfortable chair, a polished wood dresser and built-in wardrobes. The bed boasted a patchwork quilt, and two clean fluffy towels were stacked on the dresser.

Flynn put down his bag, and let Helen guide him to the bathroom just down the hall.

'We all share it,' she explained, 'having turned the other one into an operating theatre. 'Majella's down the end—Gracie sleeps in her room. I'm next and Sophie is next to you.'

So that's the geography of the house, Flynn

thought, returning to the room and considering it again—considering the family who had lived in it. Majella was probably in what had been a guest room, which meant...

He opened the wardrobe doors and knew he'd guessed correctly, old books and games stacked on the topmost shelf—a boy's books and games.

Jeff's books and games.

Flynn sank into the chair and rested his head in his hands.

Was he jealous?

He considered it carefully but knew it wasn't jealousy he was feeling. More a kind of kinship with the boy who'd owned the games—or with the man he had become.

And inside his head he made a promise—to the boy and to the man—promised him he'd never be forgotten—that he'd share their lives— then he thanked him, still silently, still communing in some way with a man he hadn't known, thanking him for watching over Majella when everyone she'd known had failed her.

She wore a dark red dress and looked so beautiful he couldn't breathe, yet somehow he'd driven to the restaurant, responding to her conversation rationally. At least, he hoped he'd sounded rational.

But now they were there, seated across from each other at a table set, as his had been, with crystal and silver. A single red rosebud in a fine crystal vase stood between them, the velvety, almost black petals matching the colour of Majella's dress.

'I can't sustain an entire evening's conversation saying nothing but "I love you,"' he said, 'but that's all I can think to say. That and "You're beautiful". Do you think if I keep repeating them you'll get bored with me?'

'Never,' she assured him, 'but you don't have to carry the conversational burden all alone you know. I might have things to say.'

'Like "I love you" and "You're beautiful"?' he said hopefully, and she chuckled and shook her head.

'Not more important than those two things, but I do love you and you are, well, if not beautiful, very handsome, but I've been thinking.'

Dread began to filter into Flynn's cocoon of happiness.

'Not bad things,' Majella assured him, reading his concern with ease.

Then she smiled, and reached out for his hands, needing to hold them while she talked.

They were interrupted by a waiter, offering a choice of drinks, then had to read the menus and make more choices. The entrees arrived far too quickly, meaning there was food to discuss and tastes to offer to each other, so all serious conversation was set aside until the meal ended.

Which meant it was some time later Majella again captured both his hands and looked at him across the table.

'Do you think perhaps we could get married on the thirtieth of September?'

'Before the deadline?' Flynn said warily. 'You'd be happy to do that? To take the house?'

'Not exactly happy,' she explained, 'but honestly, Flynn, how stupid would it be for us to marry so as not to take it when I could do so much good with the money? I could build Helen the new lab she needs to expand her business, and she could afford to hire someone to do the marketing of the products, which would give her more time to try new recipes and experiment with different oils and essences. She has so much knowledge of native plants that she's wasted just selling the products she's already developed.'

'You *have* been thinking about it,' Flynn said, smiling at her enthusiasm.

She nodded, then continued.

'There are your sisters, too. They'll need houses if they don't already have them, or we could pay off their mortgages if they do, and your mother—is she comfortable enough? We don't have to throw the money away, but we could use it where it does most good.'

'So, after all, you're marrying me for the money?'

Majella smiled at him.

'Have you paid the bill?'

He nodded.

'Then come outside and we'll find a quiet corner of the car park and I'll show you again why I'm marrying you,' she said, her heart racing as she thought of kissing Flynn again— remembering how good it always was—thinking that it could only get better as their relationship developed and their love grew stronger.

And as she kissed him she whispered things she hoped he wanted to hear, whispered her love for him that had begun when she'd been young, and how somehow a little kernel of it had stayed intact throughout the years until they'd met again, when it had burst open and blossomed into something so wondrous she had no words to describe it—no way to explain it.

Except to say, 'I love you, Flynn!'

MEDICAL™

 *Large Print*

Titles for the next six months…

December

SINGLE FATHER, WIFE NEEDED — Sarah Morgan

THE ITALIAN DOCTOR'S PERFECT FAMILY — Alison Roberts

A BABY OF THEIR OWN — Gill Sanderson

THE SURGEON AND THE SINGLE MUM — Lucy Clark

HIS VERY SPECIAL NURSE — Margaret McDonagh

THE SURGEON'S LONGED-FOR BRIDE — Emily Forbes

January

SINGLE DAD, OUTBACK WIFE — Amy Andrews

A WEDDING IN THE VILLAGE — Abigail Gordon

IN HIS ANGEL'S ARMS — Lynne Marshall

THE FRENCH DOCTOR'S MIDWIFE BRIDE — Fiona Lowe

A FATHER FOR HER SON — Rebecca Lang

THE SURGEON'S MARRIAGE PROPOSAL — Molly Evans

February

THE ITALIAN GP'S BRIDE — Kate Hardy

THE CONSULTANT'S ITALIAN KNIGHT — Maggie Kingsley

HER MAN OF HONOUR — Melanie Milburne

ONE SPECIAL NIGHT... — Margaret McDonagh

THE DOCTOR'S PREGNANCY SECRET — Leah Martyn

BRIDE FOR A SINGLE DAD — Laura Iding

MILLS & BOON®
Pure reading pleasure

1107 LP 2P P1 Medical

MEDICAL™

 *Large Print*

March

THE SINGLE DAD'S MARRIAGE WISH	Carol Marinelli
THE PLAYBOY DOCTOR'S PROPOSAL	Alison Roberts
THE CONSULTANT'S SURPRISE CHILD	Joanna Neil
DR FERRERO'S BABY SECRET	Jennifer Taylor
THEIR VERY SPECIAL CHILD	Dianne Drake
THE SURGEON'S RUNAWAY BRIDE	Olivia Gates

April

THE ITALIAN COUNT'S BABY	Amy Andrews
THE NURSE HE'S BEEN WAITING FOR	Meredith Webber
HIS LONG-AWAITED BRIDE	Jessica Matthews
A WOMAN TO BELONG TO	Fiona Lowe
WEDDING AT PELICAN BEACH	Emily Forbes
DR CAMPBELL'S SECRET SON	Anne Fraser

May

THE MAGIC OF CHRISTMAS	Sarah Morgan
THEIR LOST-AND-FOUND FAMILY	Marion Lennox
CHRISTMAS BRIDE-TO-BE	Alison Roberts
HIS CHRISTMAS PROPOSAL	Lucy Clark
BABY: FOUND AT CHRISTMAS	Laura Iding
THE DOCTOR'S PREGNANCY BOMBSHELL	Janice Lynn

 **MILLS & BOON**®
Pure reading pleasure

1107 LP 2P P2 Medical